Marilyn Pavlovsky

TAINTED MAGNOLIA

TAINTED MAGNOLIA

Is published by – Marilyn Pavlovsky

(Other Historical Fiction Titles)
BURNING SUNSHINE
HONORABLE LIFE
THE REVEREND'S DAUGHTER
Children's books available.
Going Down Town –
Cody – Paw Pals –
Kissy & Me –
Disagreeable Dot

Dedication

Written for fun from the rooms of my mind. I dedicate this book to my beautiful children and my grandchildren. Also in loving memory of a man who flew high with eagles and nicknamed those of you who you know who, (Flossy Mae)!

Author's Notes

Realizing that reincarnation is a controversial subject, may all readers know that this book is purely fictional and written for your *entertainment only*! No part of this book is factual. This book is not intended to agree or disagree with any religion or belief system.

"Reincarnation:
Is it fact or fiction?"
Lyla was a woman in search of the answer!
She & Flossy Mae would soon know that
answer all too well.

Chapter 1

As the band played a soft sweet melody, a few dancers floated across the floor. The women were dressed in the very finest of gowns, and so noticeable was the fact that all the handsome men were dressed in wonderfully designed top coats. Their ruffled shirts stood high around their strong handsome necks.

The hostess watched her quest move about as they mingled. Some were talking. Others were laughing or dancing. Rosalie thought of how glorious it would be to be young again even if just for this one night. The young people were having such a wonderful time with white teeth showing through their bright smiles underneath the glistening oil lamps and candles. The gracious lady had spared no expense to make this a most marvelous evening. It had been so many years now since she had invited guests such as these to come to her lovely plantation home. Tonight was the night this aging lady of class was fulfilling a promise to herself. Life was going to be different from this day forward. She was determined that tonight was going to be a turning point for her.

The band began to play a most wonderful upbeat song to which about everyone got up to dance. As Miss Rosalie looked out over the crowd of her invited quests, she watched as they were moving ever so gracefully across her ballroom floor. She wondered why she had not hosted an affair such as this earlier. She had let the problems of the past and her grief take over her very soul for far too many years now. Tonight was going to be the turning point of her life. She was going to forgive and forget. She was going to live her last years without torturing herself over things that were and always had been beyond her control. Things that was over and done with many years ago. She was no longer going to cower down in her rooms and hide as if in embarrassment. She was going to hold her head up high this night and greet her neighbors and friends with a bright smile upon her face. There was nothing to be discomfited about from her stand point. She had done nothing wrong. Why had she let these problems bring her down so low for all of these years? Even so low to where she wished not to ever face the world again! Well, finally she was determined. It was high time to bury the past. It was time to renew her life and let sleeping dogs lay. She was determined to stand tall for the rest of her days.

Rosalie had done everything in her power to make this night so very special. She had invited each and every one of the most elite people living in her parish. There were judges, lawyers, doctors, ministers, plantation owners and a senator or two. She was seeing friends she had not seen in years, both her and her husbands. As Rosalie glanced around the wonderfully decorated ballroom, she realized that she had not even walked into this room since her husband had passed. A lump came up into her throat when she looked around the brightly lit room. Her eyes followed the structure of the room until they fell upon the very spot where she had requested her husband be placed for his viewing after his death. She also knew that those days were the last time any of the quests had entered these halls.

Tonight was going to be different. Tonight was a joyous occasion. Tonight everything was going to be so very perfect. The ballroom looked just as it had on many joyous occasions before. The difference being, those were the days when Rosalie would make a grand entrance with her arm locked into the arm of her husband, the handsome Colonel Winthrop Wayne. But tonight the elegant lady marched into the large ballroom by herself while trying hard to put herself in this day and time and not dwell on so many years ago. She sighed under her breath,

"Oh so many, many happier years ago!"

Rosalie reached around to control the long train of her dress. She was not the slim little lady she used to be. However, unlike so many other ladies of her age, she had not gained much weight. She had gained no more than ten pounds. Yet, those ten pounds seemed to make everything else on her body shift around. For over a week she had dug through all of her armoires looking for the perfect gown. Nothing seemed to fit anymore. Finally she had decided to have a new gown tailored to fit. She had chosen a deep green fabric for the special dress she needed for this night.

As Rosalie walked gracefully deeper into the ballroom, she gazed over the large crowd. She knew that all eyes were upon her. Her eyes went straight up, as if there was a magnet on the large oil painting of the couple who still graced the large space above the fireplace. The top of the frame came within ten feet of the 33 foot ceilings in this room. The painting was of her and her husband. This large painting was painted shortly after Winthrop was given the title of Colonel. In this painting the handsome Colonel was dressed in full uniform. Rosalie was in an elegant velvet deep wine colored dress. Curls of dark brown hair dropped from the pinned up high hair style. As the aging lady stared at the painting she reached up and twisted one of those same kinds of curls around her finger. The difference was now that the curls were no longer brown. Instead they were now grey. That innocent young girl in that picture had her eyes glistening as she looked lovingly up at her tall handsome husband.

After much reminiscing, finally the refined lady's eyes dropped back into reality as she looked around the large room. She realized that she had been drinking in all of its glamour as if this were her very first time to view such splendor. She smiled at the crowd; then she let her eyes linger once again for an extended amount of time upon that beautiful painting. She was having a hard time keeping her thoughts where they should be tonight. Her thoughts just seemed to want to wonder back to the days gone by and to ponder over the things that happened to that most handsome young couple. Shaking her head as if to come out of her deep concentration, a lighter thought crossed her mind and a smile came across her face,

"Was I ever that young?"

Rosalie realized that she was enchanted by her own home, even after all of these years. She could not help but to let her eyes move ever so slowly about the room. Long, elegant, wine colored wool drapes fell from the very top of the room. They were lined in linen. They were thick, strong and beautifully tailored to fall loosely upon the shinning floor. Large square pieces of glass made up the most beautiful large windows. The windows also came close to the top of the room, then ending just a very few inches from the floor at the bottom. Elegant, superb and fitting was every item in this room. Large chairs befitting a queen graced the outer walls. Carved stone based tables were placed about. A first walk into this massive room could take one's breath away.

Rosalie had often stood in awe of this decorative ballroom during her younger years. This was a room she and her husband had designed. Most of the credit had to go her husband. He had ordered glass from some distant state. He had ordered marble and stone from back east. The whole house was built quickly, however some special items had taken sometimes years to arrive. The reaction she was getting from her emotions this night made her think that she needed to take a special day and walk all through the house. She knew there were most likely twenty rooms she had not walked inside of for years. She could remember how she used to walk down the very long halls, if for no other reason than to gaze at this beautiful ballroom. She had admired it so. After the death of the Colonel, her heart became too heavy to bring herself to approach the large double doors that kept this room separate from the rest of the large house. But tonight she was very pleased that she had gotten the courage to give this party and once more walk through these large wooden doors.

While Rosalie was soaking in her memories, a beautiful young lady twirled past her and smiled. She knew that the smile was that of thanks and appreciation.

"What a lovely young girl!"
Rosalie thought. The charming miss was being led in the grips of her strong handsome partner as he directed her around the outside of the ballroom

floor. Her head was thrown back while a large and beautiful smile looked as if it were frozen upon her pretty face. She had long dark raven colored hair that fell to the middle of her back. It was shining brightly from the bright lights of the room.

Rosalie had noticed this lovely creature right from the start of the party. As she watched the pretty girl, memories flooded her very soul. Watching this girl having such a wonderful time was bringing back every happy memory of her own past. She smiled and realized that this was a good thing. This evening most likely would accomplish exactly what she had hoped. Rosalie had been dwelling too much on the bad memories and not leaving room in her hurting heart to remember the pleasant and happy times. Watching this girl seemed to be having a healing effect on the sad Mrs. Wayne.

Rosalie could not keep her eyes off of the charming young creature. The girl looked as if it were *she* in her younger days. This young lady was causing Rosalie to truly remember her youth. She made a mental note that she must ask someone as to whom this lovely creature was. She looked over the crowd, but immediately her attention fell back with a gaze at the pretty dress the young lady had chosen for the ball. It was one that Rosalie would have chosen for herself. What a beautiful combo! What a beautiful girl all dressed up in her wine colored velvet gown that was not that much of a different look than the one she herself was wearing in that painting. Rosalie chucked within herself when she thought of how the pretty young lady was wearing her handsome escort upon her arm as if he were some sort of a trophy. The young man did not seem to mind at all. He was completely engrossed in this young lady's charms.

Finally the dance had stopped. The servants served drinks to the honored guest until they had served each person of this large crowd. Rosalie had been sure to provide a crisp white dress for the now aging servant lady Flossy Mae. As she stood against the wall noticing that her guests were enjoying all of the fineries she had offered them this night; different ladies and gentlemen were coming over to her and speaking for a while. Many wanted to thank her for such a lovely evening. There had been no parties of such for so many years at this mansion. Since the Colonel had passed, Rosalie knew that she had allowed herself to become some sort of a recluse. She was not sure of what this evening would bring. All she knew was that she now wished to come back amongst the living and welcome her friends and family once more into her home.

Flossy Mae came up to Rosalie and offered her a drink. Rosalie noticed that she did not have to force a smile tonight when she took the drink and said thank you to the servant lady. She had met the servant girl Flossy Mae on the very day of her first arrival at the Colonel's plantation. The plantation was to be her new wedded home. The slave girl was at the young age of sixteen at that time. She had already been under training to be a house servant upon Rosalie's arrival at the plantation. This slave girl would be the one chosen to care for the new Mrs. Wayne. The date she was remembering was the date of her marriage to one of the most sought after men in her part of the country. She had married the rich and the most powerful man who would later be known as the great Colonel Winthrop Jacob Wayne.

As Flossy Mae floated gracefully through the large group of people, Rosalie could feel that old resentment flowing through her veins. Both women were in their sixties by now. The Colonel had been gone for over ten years. Old problems had been forgiven and buried. At least that is what everyone wanted to believe. Yet they were still not forgotten. Rosalie could not help but notice that the old slave woman still had that curvy figure. Nor had age hindered that carved out beautiful looking face.

Rosalie was always told that she was a very handsome woman. She knew that she was. Coming from the blue blood of Louisiana she had also been groomed very well. Her destiny from childhood was to marry well. Her marriage to Winthrop Jacob Wayne was almost a planned affair by the two sets of parents. During later years, the Colonel and Rosalie had talked of this often. They decided that it would have been regretful for either of them to have married anyone else.

Rosalie was never sure as to whether she had been in love with the Colonel when she married him, or whether she was only infatuated with his station in life. She knew he was probably the most handsome man in her parish. She also knew she had fallen very deeply in love with this man shortly after their wedding.

The couple enjoyed the first years of their marriage. They also had two children fairly early in the marriage. After the last child was born, Rosalie fell very ill one summer morning and was bed rested for the rest of that year. After that date, she and her husband realized that they were now unable to conceive. There would be no more children born into the all-powerful Wayne family. This broke the Colonel's heart. He had so wanted a large family. It was as if neither knew the reasons why, but within a couple of years the husband and wife became distant with each other.

Colonel Wayne spent most of his days out in the fields with the slaves, while Rosalie entertained herself with her elite friends and family. She tried to win the affections of her beloved husband back, but there seemed to always be some road block or a reason why she could not. It took Rosalie many, many years to figure out the reason why she could never win. For years, she had blamed herself for not being able to give the Colonel more children, a most wanted son and the large family he so desired.

Rosalie had also been saddened for so many years because of another terrible loss. This big loss had contributed much to her sadness and she had since built up a big wall around herself. A most horrible tragedy had caused an even larger distance between the Colonel and Mrs. Wayne. When the couple's youngest daughter Vivian was but ten years of age, a tragedy struck their home. The little girl loved being in the upstairs of the big old mansion. The winding stairway ended atop with a large room sized landing. Although it was tough for the previous generation to have gotten large items up the stairs; a massive grand piano type instrument was placed at the very top upon that large landing. Their lovely daughter Vivian had loved to play this instrument and she played it beautifully. Her instructor came only once per week, but she would spend many hours practicing. Music seemed to be her passion.

One evening a lit oil lamp had tumbled off of the top of the large piano like instrument and had rolled down the steps. Possibly Vivian had bumped into it or something! The glass lamp had shattered with the very first bang. It was a large, fully filled oil lamp and flames followed with every spill. Before anyone could get up the stairs to help Vivian, the beautiful carpeted staircase was engulfed in flames. No one could save precious little Vivian on that day. The family and the servants had to reluctantly run outside of the house to take cover under a large magnolia tree. They watched as the large yellow house was burning. Nothing could be done. The large wood framed home burned to the ground within minutes.

Sadly the Colonel and Rosalie did their mourning separately. Their home was quickly rebuilt. The plantation continued to be a busy operation. Rosalie mourned in her bedroom for months on end while the Colonel mourned all over the fields and the barns. The oldest daughter Louise was left to mourn the loss all alone. Her parents were lost in their own grief and lost from each other and her. The family had become most isolated from each other.

Louise was a constant friend to Flossy Mae. She had grown up under the servant woman's feet. Thank God, Flossy Mae had been there for poor Louise during all of her times of need. Flossy Mae had mothered this young girl through the grief of losing her little sister and the need for the loving care of her parents. The parents, who were consumed in grief, had hidden inside of themselves. Flossy Mae was a rock of strength for

16

the sad young girl.   She became more than a servant to Louise.

There were of course, stations in life that could not be ignored. Flossy Mae was a slave and Louise was a young lady of class. Miss Louise must always keep her superiority over the slave lady. There were many times when the young girl would be firm and uncaring in front of others, only to apologize to Flossy Mae in private. This world seemed to be such a mixed up and turned upside down world to live in.   It could be so very confusing for a loving child when it came to these stations in life.

Flossy Mae was very intelligent.   At one time Rosalie had taken much interest in the education of this house slave. Rosalie had taught the young wench to read and write.   She had trained her right alongside of her own daughters. The old master mum Charlotte was still alive at that time and she much disapproved of the training of a slave in this manner. She would tell of how in most areas it was even against the law to teach a slave how to read and write. Rosalie was not sure that she was doing the training out of the kindness of her heart or from the need to prove something to the Colonel's old hard headed mother. Little did she know as the years passed by; Rosalie would live to regret her kindness.

C hapter 2

During the next century, in the years of the 1980's and the 1990's, a woman named Lyla J. Wilson was going about her daily duties. Lyla had often traveled throughout the southern part of the United States. She would travel for her company often. On one such occasion, she remembered waking up suddenly while riding through a small rural area of Louisiana. The braking the driver of car had done due to someone driving improperly in front of him had caused her abrupt awakening. After seeing what had happened; Lyla, while still in a sleepy faze, looked out of the side window. She saw the most beautiful large old plantation home off in the distance. This home was so very large. It had pillars two stories high. The pillars went all of the way around the front and the sides of this large home. This house seemed so very far off of the highway. Lyla felt sorry for the lovely old house. Like so many beautiful old southern mansions, this one had been left to deteriorate all by itself. Lyla made a remark to her riding partner about the sadness of it all. He answered by saying,

"Lyla, I know how much you love those old homes. That house does not seem to have a driveway up to it anymore. If it did, and I thought we were not trespassing I would drive you right up there to see it. But it is sitting out in the middle of that field. It looks like there are several hundred acres around it, but there does not look like there is even a road up to it anymore."

Lyla thanked her partner for his concern then mourned the loss of such beauty. Even from the modern four lane highway she could see this beautiful home was falling down. How sad, how very sad! She remarked about the sorry people who may have inherited such property and complained that those people could not see the importance of keeping the history and the loveliness of this home alive.

Lyla, being born and raised in the western part of the United States could not visualize how anyone could ever let a place like that fall down. She would have given anything to have owned and lived in a beautiful home like that. After much grumbling to her working peer, she puffed up her pillow, dropped her head heavily upon it and fell back to sleep. She knew she must sleep for a while before it became her turn to drive.

The two management employees of a large sales firm had traveled to Louisiana from the State of North Carolina. The trip was to train a few new employees in a newly opened office. Many such trips were made throughout the south by a management team per year. Lyla usually traveled this route to Louisiana only once per year. These trips were most usually accomplished by way of flight. This time it was done in road travel fashion because the trip had many stops along the way. The two were to stop in each state, either on their way to their last stop or on their way home. They were to visit each of their company offices along their path. These driving trips could be most tiring.

Lyla started dreaming almost instantly after falling back to sleep. The dream seemed so realistic! So vivid! She felt she was personally in this dream. However, she was most shocked that she was only a seven year old child. She could see herself standing under a rusty tin roofed porch. The porch went the full length across the front of a worn wood looking shack. The boards on this long house were of a weathered dark brown. Not one drop of paint had ever been placed upon this house. Under the little girl's feet were many stones. The round and oblong stones were placed very closely together, obviously to make a more solid surface. Each stone was from four to eight inches across. Every stone had a smooth finish and the darkness under this porch roof caused the stones to be very cold underneath her bare feet.

Lyla looked up above her head while in her dream and realized that draped from porch post to porch post were grape vines. This was another reason for the coolness under this darkened porch. When she looked down, she realized she was wearing a long dress hitting between her ankles and her knees. The dress had very small flowers embroidered distant and haphazardly upon it. The dress did not seem to have much of a color to it. It was of a tea or a tan like color. The threads used to make the embroidered flowers were not much darker than the dress and looked as if a child may have been practicing how to do such things. Lyla only knew the style of the dress was that of many, many years ago. As the little girl stood upon the cold stones, her hand and arm were stretched out to hold onto one of the full length porch posts. Lyla stayed completely aware of the cold stones underneath her feet.

The car came to a stop. Lyla awakened with the hopes of being refreshed. It was her turn to drive. However, the dream during her nap had taken its toll on her. She felt drained! She could not help but question why a dream could feel so very real. She also questioned as to why the dream could wear her out this way.

At the stop, Lyla got a cup of coffee. She had a long road trip ahead of her and it would be several hours before they could stop at a motel for their night's rest. Once the couple was back on the road and the other employee had fallen asleep, the shaken lady started analyzing her dream. She could not get that dream out of her head. She tried! She somehow felt the dream had something to do with that beautiful old house that she had just seen a few hours ago, so she needed to get her head around something else.

Finally, after hours of thinking and trying to figure out the dream along many miles of highway, Lyla pulled the car into a motel parking lot. The night at the motel did not seem to help very much either. Thankfully within a few days the business at hand would be taken care of. A full day tomorrow and the next were planned. The employees would then start their long journey back to the main office on that following morning where they would continue with their respective positions.

Both Lyla and her working partner were up for promotions. This was very exciting. Lyla loved her job. She would often pinch herself to see if she really did hold this wonderful position. It was so exciting. It was filled with travel and meeting new people. The pay was fabulous and the prestige could not be matched in any other way according to Lyla's way of thinking. She knew she was good at her job and she started each day with total bliss, happiness and confidence.

Once back in North Carolina, while doing her normal duties and living her normal life, Lyla had all but forgotten her dream. She had mentioned to her coworkers how she felt about that beautiful old plantation house that she had seen. She told of the shame of losing this beautiful history, but the dream had all but faded away. Oh, but that was not to last. One night just a few weeks into being in the comfort of her home, it all came rushing back.

Lyla had talked with her children a little while before she had retired to her bedroom. She thought she might read some on the new novel she had purchased while in Louisiana. She pulled the book out and read the back cover once again. This time she noticed the story was one of those romance novels. The kind that only tells of the damsel in distress, then the handsome knight comes to her rescue. Then they all live happily ever after. She was not fond of this kind of a book. God knows she had read a million just like it. Whatever possessed her to buy that thing anyway? Just the same, she thought she would start reading it while knowing that reading anything would put her to sleep. For sure, she did not get past the first two pages until she was fast asleep.

Shortly after falling asleep, Lyla had a most real dream again. In this dream she was standing on that very same porch. She was once again just seven years old. Even while dreaming, she wondered how she would know that she was seven years old. Once more her dress was long and she was barefooted. She could once again feel the cold stones underneath her feet. She could see the muscadine grapes falling from the timbers above her. They wrapped around each timber post. She

23

could smell the smells. The grapes were ripe and they had a most amazing odor about them. Lyla was not sure that she had ever smelled muscadines before and made a mental note of that fact even while she was still in the dream.

This dream seemed to be completely real and it was as if it were happening in real time. Lyla sat straight up in her bed awakening forcefully! She realized quickly that this did not feel like an ordinary dream. It was more of a vision. What on earth was going on? What forces were causing such a thing to happen to her? Was she losing her mind? She knew many of her family members seemed to have an ESP manner about them. They could often tell something happening in the future and so on, but she never seemed to have much of that ability. Besides, this dream was of the past. Lord, it was of way, way back in the past.

Lyla looked across her body to see that the duck feathered filled comforter was still in place covering her feet. She was trying to rationalize each part of her dream. If her feet had been uncovered and coldness had befallen them, then she would feel that she had dreamed the dream just because her feet were cold. She tried to think of anyone from her past who could have owned a porch such as the one in her dream, or a house such as the old shack in the dream. She tried to remember if she had watched something on TV that could have triggered such behavior, but nothing came to mind. Lyla had what people would call a strong continuing memory. She never forgot anything. So, she was pretty sure that there was nothing in her past that could be causing her to remember such things. She was just as sure that she had never seen a dress made in that fashion. She had a hunch that this little dress had to come from somewhere in the 1700's or maybe the early 1800's.

The next morning Lyla felt drained once more. She did not quite understand this because she had not stayed awake and dwelled upon the subject. She was more level headed than that. She knew that her job and her children were of most importance. She had the ability to shame herself for any unnecessary worry about frivolous things. Yet, she was extremely tired from the experience of this dream. She also could not remove it from her mind. She felt the same as she had the last time when she had dreamed this very same dream. She was weary as though she had run a marathon, climbed a mountain or something of that nature. She was completely exhausted!

More months passed and once again Lyla had all but forgotten her crazy dreams. There were times while alone that the dream would pop into her mind for a brief period. She would pass it off while questioning herself as to why it felt so important to her. She even did some research on the computer while checking out the clothing of different periods. She had found her hunch to be correct. The dress she had seen in her dreams was from the latter part of the seventeen hundreds and the early eighteen hundreds. She also found similar elongated houses. These houses were also from that same period. The homes were those of a poorer class of people. They were homes of poor migrates or slaves. Most often in the Southern United States, these were the homes of the slaves. The homes were most usually built upon a master or landowner's property to house one or another kind of worker. This information seemed to satisfy Lyla's curiosity to where she now believed that she most have read about these things in a book somewhere. Being the history buff that she was, this was a plausible reason for the unnerving dreams.

A year had passed and once again it was time for the manager to visit her satellite offices. These trips were often done for many reasons. The trips were made for the training of new employees, or for a yearly review of other employees. Once again, Lyla found herself headed to Louisiana. This time she was going to fly. Once she arrived and tended to her business, she was then to rent a car and stop off at each office on her way back to North Carolina. This year's trip would be handled alone.

Business at several offices of Louisiana was finally completed. The reviews were given and socializing with other employees was complete. Lyla knew that hearing of the employees grievances or of their satisfaction was all in a day's work. With the completion of so many stops and duties, the working lady had many things to think about on her long drive home. Evenings were spent with an open briefcase and room service meals upon a bed. There was so much business upon Lyla's mind, but she was also anxious to get home. She had spoken with her children many times while on this trip. Although her children were quite sufficient young adults by now; Lyla could not help but worry when she was away from home. She also missed them very much. Her children were her blessings. The children were the only truly wonderful things in her life. Love and marriage had not been a lasting deal for this charming lady. But, her beautiful children were a constant. They were her heart and she hated to be away from them.

With all of these things crossing Lyla's mind while she was driving, she was shocked when she got a strange deja`vu feeling. We all have recollections of a deja`vu experience. The word means 'already seen'. It is that eerie feeling that we've been in a place, or walked down a street before actually being there. It almost always seems as if we are reliving a dream. So, one can imagine the feelings poor Lyla was experiencing. She topped a hill and came down under some power lines. Evening was coming in and the sky was beautifully colored in pinks, purples and yellows. In the distance, Lyla could see she was approaching still another hill. In this large valley something was overtaking her very being. She had traveled this road before, of course! Now was her second time, but she was not exactly sure where she was on the map. All of a sudden she looked to her right and was shocked almost out of her wits at what she saw. She was directly in front of that beautiful old mansion she had seen on her last trip, and it was still standing! It was more shattered than before, but it was still standing in all of its majesty.

Lyla came to a screeching halt. She pulled the rental car off to the curb of the road. Her hands were shaking as she gathered her composer enough to get out of the car. What could cause these feelings? How strange the deja`vu feeling! Then once she topped that hill she was in the very same spot of that beautiful old house. It was as if that old house was trying to talk to her. Something, someone or that old house had some

27

sort of a nerve shattering power over her. She knew for a fact that there is no way that she would have known this house was just over that hill because she had been asleep on her last trip. She was asleep up until the time her partner had hit the brakes. That did not happen until they were deep into the valley and right in front of that old mansion. Suddenly she got crazy with her thoughts; as weird as these happenings seemed to be, was there a ghost trying to talk with her?

Lyla tried to regain her composure while stopped in the middle of nowhere along the side of a busy traveled highway.

"Foolishness…!"

she laughed! She did not believe in such things! She was way too educated to ever believe in anything so silly. Yet, something was so very, very strange. Finally, she gathered herself together enough to decide whether to go on up the highway like any sensible adult would do, or to get out and survey her surroundings. She decided to do the latter.

While looking up towards that beautiful old plantation home, Lyla noticed something else in the distance. It was placed far below the mansion and almost completely covered by trees and overgrowth.

"Oh – My - God!"

Thought Lyla!

"There's my house!"

Nestled deep within the large overgrowths, Lyla could see an elongated cabin type home. It was covered in vines, but she could still see the outlines of the house. The large timber porch posts were still very visible and they stretched the full length of the long porch. An old rusty tin roof had fallen in, but much of the old planked up and down wood was still visible upon the walls.

Lyla walked down the embankment a ways and just stood there in disbelief. The longer she stood there, the more strange things seemed to be. Suddenly she realized that a problem had developed in her believing that everything could be coincidental. One major problem being that this elongated house could not have been seen from the cars moving up above. One would have to be out of their car and standing on the embankment as she stood this very minute before they could ever get a glimpse of this site to behold.

Okay, now Lyla was getting scared. What the Hell could this all mean? She was suddenly trembling with tears flowing down her face. Why was she so sad? Why did this place make her want to cry? She knew that she felt badly because beautiful places like this were left to fall down, but this pain felt so deep within her very soul. What so terrible had happened upon this spot? How was a woman from the modern years involved in anyway? The only thing this statuses business woman, standing there dressed in her business suit and high heels, was certain of was that this was entirely too real. Too freaky real! Real *__what__* was the question?

Lyla just knew she was having some paranormal experience that she could not understand and it was scaring the wits out of her! She stood on that bank for a long time while trying to sort out her feelings and to just understand. She felt safety in the fact that modern day people were above. Modern day people were driving their modern day cars along that modern day highway. She knew that she should get back into one of those modern day cars and leave right now, but she felt glued to that spot. She told herself if it got to the point that she could no longer hear those modern day cars, well then she was sure that she was totally doomed! She reminded herself to be aware of that fact. Should that happen, she must run as fast as she could back to her car!

When there seemed to be no rational reasoning for anything, Lyla climbed back up the embankment, got back into her car and continued on her way. Once again, just as last year, the business trip ended and Lyla went on with her daily duties of being a mother and a manager. Thoughts of that evening in Louisiana would always haunt the pretty lady, but she refused to let it control her life. Possibly on her next year's trip to those offices she would inquire about that old plantation. With that idea in mind, she put her thoughts back upon a shelf and never spoke of them to anyone in the months that followed.

C hapter 3

The year was now 2010, the whole world was worried. People were losing their jobs and their homes. Middle class people had all but vanished and nothing but worry could be seen upon everyone's faces. 2012 was supposed to be the end of the world according to the predictions of old. Still, most people wanted to live their lives to the fullest. Lyla was no exception to that rule. By these years, Lyla's life was pretty much miserable most of the time. Her children had grown and had flown the coop as so many would say. Oh, they kept their mother informed of their lives while reporting from many states away. They visited when they could, but their mother had so many lonely days in between.

So, Lyla did not seem to be too overly concerned as to whether the world crumbled down around her or not! The poor lady was now in her late forties. She had been through many ups and downs in her life. Unhappiness had not always been the case, but as of right now it seemed to consume a large part of her life. She had read somewhere that in history her condition of depression was considered to be a sin. It was contributed to a demon by the name of Sloth. To Lyla it didn't matter much if it were a sin or not because she could not prevent feeling the way that she did. She felt life had cheated her and she stayed in a dark state of depression just about all of the time.

The beautiful lady had once met the man of her dreams. She married him and life was bliss! Complete bliss! This man in her life treated her like she was his queen. He spoiled her. He took her to exotic places all around the world. He told her every day that she was beautiful. He made constant love to her and the two basked in a deep fulfilling love. They had three beautiful children whom they both completely adored.

Years passed in Lyla's life. Her children grew up. They went to college. They got careers and they got married. They had beautiful grandchildren for the charming Lyla to enjoy. She was always thankful for her many blessings. One of those blessings that brought her so much happiness was the fact that she had met the man of her dreams. She was so very thankful for that and felt when saddened that she must be more appreciative of that fact. She had married this beautiful man to live happily ever after. She had delighted in the pleasures of her family. On the work front she was very happy as well. Lyla received many promotions. She traveled all over the world with her handsome husband and her life was grand. Life was very, very good! Any problems she may have had in the past or if she even had any, seemed to be just that, the past! When she thought of her past young years it was as if she was thinking of someone else's life not hers, because she had found complete Heaven. In Lyla's way of thinking, her life was next to perfect!

Even with all of this happiness, life can be very, very cruel at times and especially cruel when it came to Lyla. In the later years she had been drawn down by deaths of family and loved ones, both young and old. Then at this fairly young age Lyla had lost her love, her happiness, her other half. Her husband had died unexpectedly and almost instantly. Lyla was devastated and knew not where to turn. Her life was turned upside down when her beloved husband passed away so quickly. He had a car wreck one evening on his way home from work. One would have believed he had died from the car accident, but Lyla was told that his heart had ruptured and that caused the accident! She was never quite sure how she survived the days after her husband's death. After much grief, she seemed to just wake up one day doomed to be in a deep dark place for the rest of her life. She was now *all alone!* She was now living distances away from her loving children. They had their own lives. Lyla knew that they must go to where profits were the best for them and their families. She hated the fact that each child lived many states away from her.

After her husband's death, Lyla had retired from her much loved sales manager position and took up a new career at her middle age. She had decided to change her life completely. She decided to sell her house and move. It did not matter where she moved to, she just wanted to change her life and get away from all of her memories and the pain. She thought she would try somewhere colder. The south could get so very hot anymore at the end of the summers. So, she took a position in a northern state.

Silly as this may sound to a rational thinking person, Lyla thought it would be fun to wear winter boots and winter coats. She had also heard if one lived in the north, one would not wrinkle nearly as fast. Something about that cold weather kept your skin preserved in some way! She knew this all to be nonsense, but she had nothing better to do than try a new state. There were other reasons for choosing the state that she chose. She would be between her children and traveling to see them would be so much easier. Then she had a brother who had moved there years and years ago because his wife was from that particular state. Actually, once Lyla landed a job, she felt very fortunate for receiving another high paying position. It was a fairly decent position and she was still young enough to receive two retirements when the time came for her to retire. This second position was not nearly as demanding as the first. It did not take the brain power or the hours that the first position had required. But, it was not nearly as exciting either.

Suddenly, Lyla found much time on her hands. She had time she did not need. She had too much time to feel sorry for herself. She was never much for long term relationships with anyone except her loving family. Many considered her a snob. She knew she was not a snob, she just wasn't sure that she trusted other people that far! But, she also knew she did not know how to relate with most normal people. Management had caused this isolation. She knew that to be a fact. One could not be best friends with their employees. If their employees were the only people that they had time to associate with, then there could not be much of a long term or deep relationships there. It was always,

"She's the boss; I'm the employee mentality."

Lyla began going to church in her new northern state and started to meet new people. She took up ballroom dancing as a hobby and she read continually. As a working woman, she tried to bury herself in her work and her hobbies.

34

Although this woman never believed that she could ever want another man, after a few years Lyla was once more on the dating scene. Still thin, tall and very attractive, there was not a problem attracting prospective mates. But, in her younger years there had always been a major problem with Lyla. This lady had a magnet on her when it came to attracting losers. This was an old trait from her college years that she had obviously never lost. She would often wonder as to how she had found her late husband. He had been someone so very special! She would never know the answer to that question. Something in the cosmic world must have gone wrong and permitted her to live in bliss for a short time. Once the forces realized that she was not supposed to be in that world, they pulled her happiness away.

Lyla was not meant to have a lifetime of happiness! This is what she now believed. Her destiny was to live in pain. She knew this to be true. She had only wished that things could change. The poor lady was living a big part of her life hoping and dreaming about a different future. She so often tried to live her life in a state of a dream world. She could picture herself in a serene atmosphere with the perfect man and the perfect home. It had come to the point to where she enjoyed that dream world more than she enjoyed the real world that she lived in. When something would snap her back into reality she would often become disappointed that she was back.

After dating a few losers, Lyla was about to give up and live the rest of her life alone. She knew the longevity of her family could mean that she might live to be one-hundred. If this be true, she would have many, many years of being alone.

For a few years Lyla stayed in the cold northern state. She did truly enjoy living there, yet she never really felt quite at home. It was nice to be able to hop over to see the children in their respective states by way of car. But, there were just too many days and nights alone. Her brother and his wife had their own life with their many family members and friends. She had not moved all that close to her brother anyway for those very reasons. She had not wanted to interfere with his settled life. She had to also drive some distance to visit with him. So, she usually did her visiting on some of the weekends.

Lyla sometimes regretted that she had quit her prestige, but stressful job in the south and taken a position of a kind to where she could go home each night and forget the workload. Still she had planned for long term employment once more. With the new position she had nothing but tons of extra time on her hands, but for what? She came home to an empty house where she was always lonely and sometimes cold. After a while she started wondering what she was even doing there. Yet, she was appreciative of the move because this place had healed some of her grieving. For that she was very thankful. But, after just a few years she knew it was time to move on.

Lyla had hoped to receive yet another retirement from the position in the north, but nothing seemed to be going as she had planned. None of her hopes had panned out. She was not the happy person she had hoped that she may be in a state where she had never lived with her husband. Nothing was new and exciting to her as she had hoped. So, she decided to migrate back to the western state of her birth. She decided on this while believing maybe being near her mother may ease some of her pain. She realized that after her husband's death that she was not very stable anymore, anywhere. She knew that was probably of her own doing. In this northern cold state she once again thought she needed a change of scenery to deal with all of her grief. She often felt like a fish out of water. Moving closer to her mother just might help. As for her children, she never traveled that much to see them anyway. Then a flippant thought crossed her mind when she said aloud,

"The last time I checked Lyla, there were still airplanes!"

So, another move was planned for the now unstable Miss Lyla. Once she arrived in Nevada, she did not have the luck that she had hoped for in finding a position. Two factors played a part in this scenario. She was past the hiring age of young management candidates. Number two, her mother's area was small and very few jobs were to be found. She started working at many different office positions. Most of them were temporary. She would take about anything to pay her bills. Finally she landed a receptionist position for a construction company in a small neighboring city. This was still close enough to her mother, yet far enough away if anyone can understand that way of thinking. She wasn't even sure that she understood this desire. The blessings to this move were that she was in her home western state surrounded by the places she knew and fond memories of her childhood. She felt that she was there to stay for the rest of her days. She could grow old in the comfort of home now. Obviously she was going to live the rest of her life alone, so she might as well be home to do that. Then she would think of morbid thoughts when she would say to herself,

"This will be so much easier for my children. They will not have to pay out of their inheritance or insurance money to move me all of the way across the country to bury me at home!" Now if those thoughts did not come from a deep dark depression, she had never heard of depression.

Lyla worked and cared for her mother for the next two years, but as so many things that had happened to Lyla without her control; just when she thought that all hope was gone in ever having a meaningful relationship with a man again, it happened. One day while on her low paying, non-meaningful job, Lyla noticed a tall handsome man walking into her office. She had not seen one so handsome in many, many years. Meeting a tall handsome stranger was not on her agenda. She did not need this right now! But, one look and she was hooked! She knew she wanted to meet this man! Oh Lyla knew that she was a big sucker for the extreme handsome man. Well the sucker part surfaced because the extreme in that sentence meant this man was the EXTREME handsome. Suddenly everything seemed extreme! This was an extreme weakness of hers.

Lyla knew this sort of attraction only happened when she was not happy. She was always true to her mate. No matter who that person may have been; husband or a friend. She really did not notice handsome men when they were around her if she was in a relationship. She obviously wore some sort of blinders! But, let her be alone and let one come along, she could be easily fascinated. She could also be easily swayed if asked for a date. She would usually think the worst of that handsome man first in her book of knowledge, but she always hoped for the best. Like most every woman would or should, she did enjoy the company of a handsome man.

The minute the tall dark handsome stranger walked into the door and spoke; Lyla heard a beautiful southern accent. She melted! Meeting a tall handsome **_SOUTHERN_** stranger was definitely not on her agenda right now. She did not need this right now! Not in this time and in this place. She was home! She was home to stay! She had resolved herself to live out the rest of her years awaiting death in the place of her birth. She would never let any man cause her to leave her home again. Never! Ever! Never Again! **_But_** that accent and the stranger's very, very good looks were really working on her!

If anyone else had been in that room, Lyla may have walked off and never listened to a word this man had to say. But she was alone! She figured that she was going to become more hooked with each word that came out of this marvelous looking man's mouth. These feelings were not just coming from his good looks and accent. There seemed to be something very special about this man's voice. Add that smooth southern drawing accent and Lyla could feel herself shivering clear to her bones. This made the thoroughly mature, usually sensible woman think in jest,

"I would follow you anywhere big boy!"
She laughed at her school girl thoughts and realized how silly she was being. She would follow no one anywhere! Besides, this man was surely married or one of those worst kinds that she always seemed to attract.

Lyla's marriage, while being married to a wonderful southern man had caused her to live most of her life in the southern part of the United States. She was very happy in the south with her children, her home and her husband. The south had become her home and she had once believed that she would live there forever. She hoped that the southern feelings that were imbedded within her were the only reasons for this man having the effect he was having upon her this very minute.

Leaving the south several years ago, Lyla would not expect to hear the lovely sound of a southerner in the Western United States. Days of the more gentle speaking and slower ways were days of the past for Lyla. Yet, today this handsome stranger was most surely from the *Deep, Deep South*. With Lyla's migration north, then her move back to Nevada, hearing this southern accent was a most pleasant surprise! She knew she was being really silly being so fascinated when in reality she was just very happy to hear a beautiful southern accent once more. She had missed that beautiful accent during these past years.

The words were coming out slowly and so smoothly from the mouth of this very tall and handsome man. He was big muscled and broad shouldered. He had dark waving hair and bright blue eyes. Suddenly Lyla felt the most home feeling from just being close to this gentleman. To be a stranger, she felt an extreme closeness to this man. She could tell from the man's stare that he was having the same feelings about her.

After the initial shock of the southern accent, within seconds Lyla started feeling that she had met this man before. How weird was that?

Yet she believed that there was no way that she could have ever met this tall man before. She smiled as she thought,

"Now I would have most definitely remembered something like that!'

Yet, questions started clouding her brain. Had she seen this man before? Why did it feel as though she had known him all of her life? Analyzing herself as she always did, it most probably was the comfort zone she was feeling while being in the room with someone from the south. Even with that, she could not understand her feelings. She consoled herself by believing that it must just be that long southern draw in his voice or the fact that it had been years since she had been with a man. Yet, this man was acting strangely all of a sudden himself. He obviously felt some of the same feelings. Lyla wondered why it felt like she had just come home. Nevada was her true home. Not the south. It was also very odd that she could tell that the handsome stranger was having some of those same kinds of strange feelings. However, he was quite suave. Lyla could tell that he could cover his feelings smoothly. Just as smooth as the,

"Hello, my name is William! William T. Jenson to be exact!"

came out of his mouth, he took complete charge of the conversation while he ask a question,

"Could I interest you in going out to dinner with me tonight?"

Shock waves went up and down Lyla's spine. That was strange. Lyla was sure that this man did not come into her isolated office just to ask her to dinner. That would not have happened even in one of those romance novels that she so distasted. The following words flowed out of Lyla's mouth as if someone else was in her body. She barely realized she was talking. If so, she would have never answered so quickly. But she could hear herself saying in her own reverted Southern accent,

"Well yes, Mr. William; I would *l-o-v-e* to have dinner with you!"

As the tall man spoke awhile, he then smiled and thanked her for accepting. Then he told her who he came to see. She directed him in that direction and he disappeared into another office. Lyla sat there dumbfounded over her answer. She heard the man say that he was in town on business and was staying at the Holiday Inn on the East end of town. He had stated that they, the hotel had a most unusual restaurant in their building. He had asked the question, or maybe he had made the statement, however one might take it by saying:

"It being a week night, would it be plausible for you to meet me at that restaurant at 7:00pm this evening?"

Lyla had agreed and had shaken her head yes!

Had Lyla been in the correct state of mind she would have probably realized this man was taking complete charge. He was making decisions and expecting her to follow his directions. His good looks probably always got good results. Where was her mind? How could she be so taken in by this stranger to where she would allow such control?

Lyla was from a generation to where the women had liberated themselves. A woman such as herself, having a good education and high professional positions would never bow down to let a man control her very life. Had she been away from her professional life that long? Had she

42

dropped her guard that badly? Southern men had that reputation anyway! She had been extremely lucky with her southern husband. He had believed in equality, unlike so many old southern gentleman of the past. He had always considered Lyla to be his equal. Now, she had just accepted the wishes of a strong southern and possibly a controlling man. What was she to do now?

Work continued that day with Lyla in a confused state of mind.   She was extremely nervous, but she was also very excited. She had not been on a date in years now. Finally the, what seemly was a long work day, ended.   Lyla nervously placed her key into her car starter and headed home. She bathed quickly. She messed with her makeup until she felt it to be perfect. She then dressed in the neatest slack suit that she could find in her closet and headed for the other side of town. As she walked into the poorly lit restaurant she could see the handsome stranger nowhere about. She thought to herself,

"Great, at my age I am letting a man toy with me!"
She thought of how very handsome this man was and the fact that she knew he had been around the block more than once. He had possibly thought it was fun to set up some silly western lady for a downfall. She knew not what to believe! At one time she knew that her looks alone would have kept any man from treating her that way. She did not feel so drop dead gorgeous anymore. Gee, she was a middle aged woman now. Everyone told her that she still looked the same, but she was always quick to point out her flaws.

Time passed and Lyla was getting upset! Then she thought of how since she was already there, she might as well order a drink and relax

43

some before she totally wrote off her handsome stranger. She let the hostess seat her and she ordered a glass of white wine. A pianist was playing a beautiful song upon the piano. Lyla, being somewhat more laid back than her former self these days, decided to enjoy the atmosphere and the moment.

While the pretty lady sipped on the glass of wine she became engrossed in the music as she watched the pianist's hands move across the keys. She was not aware someone had walked in behind her chair. She became startled when her handsome stranger bent over from his tall height and placed a kiss upon her cheek. He said,

"Hi Honey, I'm home!"

Although Lyla was thoroughly aggravated with this man for almost standing her up, she laughed and said,

"I was about to give up on you!"

He then became more serious when he said,

"That would have been a tragedy because I was so looking forward to this evening."

Lyla having to wait so long had put her in a somewhat touchy mood. She frowned and said nothing. Then he said,

"I am so sorry to keep a beautiful woman such as yourself, waiting on me like this! But, business called!"

Now it was as if Lyla was setting the tone of the evening when she laughed and said,

"Sure, I will bet that business was a call from your wife!"

She saw a frown come over the handsome stranger's forehead and noticed the beautiful grey and black hair coming down into the most perfect widows peek. Now, she worried that maybe the two glasses of wine that she had during her wait had possibly gone to head. Without waiting for an answer or a remark in response to her flippant statement, she laughed out loud. She found it to be humorous that he too had a sharp widows peek the same as she. A giggly thought went through her mind. She wondered if maybe this fashionably *LATE* southern stranger was her soul mate! She laughed out loud again. Thankfully, the handsome stranger brought her back into reality when he said,

"No actually, I was busy getting a traffic ticket! It seems that your state has a seatbelt law that applies to pickup trucks the same as cars. My state does not have that rule. So far, every man on my crew has received a traffic ticket. If I did not own the company and had not gotten one myself, I guess I would be pretty mad at the whole bunch of my guys!"

With that, the big man threw his ten gallon hat upon the table and laughed a loud husky laugh as he said,

"Let's eat, I'm hungry!"

Lyla could not help but feel that comfort zone again. She noticed that both of them seemed to be in that zone. It was as if they were an old married couple who had been married all of their lives; a couple who just staggered into a restaurant for an evening's meal. She had never felt this way with anyone before, especially after just first meeting them. Was it his laid back southern manner? Was it his smooth personality? Or, was it only she who was feeling this way, possibly because she had been alone for so many years by now. Whatever it was, she was not ready to put her finger on it just yet!

As the evening progressed, the couple ordered dinner. The handsome stranger William ordered steak.

"Imagine that!"

Lyla thought. What else, would this larger than life man order, she thought with a silent laugh. He was not lying, he was hungry. He ate and he ate. Lyla had never seen such an appetite. He would clean his plate, only to look over at something left on Lyla's plate and say,

"You gone'a eat that?"

Lyla believed she had never seen anyone eat as much as he. Of course she had to take into consideration that this man was way over six foot tall, very large and strong muscled. He also obviously worked very hard and with long hours. Yes, she guesses that he would be a hungry man. While Lyla watched this large man eat in silence, she thought to herself,

"Man could I ever cook for you!"

She loved to cook and knew she would thoroughly enjoy cooking for someone who enjoyed food as much as her handsome stranger seemed to enjoy it. She also knew from the evening's conversation and from the way that William had looked at her sometimes; he would believe that she could never cook. Seemingly anyone in his book that worked the jobs that she had worked, drove the kind of car that she drove and dressed the way that she dressed must be pampered. She felt challenged. She knew right from the start that she was going to have to change Mr. William's opinion of what she could or could not do. Then she laughed to herself as she thought of how she needed to have a long talk with herself. She almost said out loud,

"Who's talking long term here? This guy is going home when his job is complete! You better enjoy this minute Miss Lyla! Have fun! Quit being such a prude!"

When William finally had his fill of dinner, he ordered more wine. This time the big man ordered a special brand of wine and asked for the whole bottle. Lyla knew this man was of the world. He may sound like a calm southern gentleman, but she could tell that he had most probably been around the world and everywhere one could go. She knew most that he had done everything there was to do. There was a strong air about him that showed that he was a man of knowledge and of wealth. She could not help but notice his lack of concern of how much anything was going to cost.

After a few glasses of wine and the telling of many stories, William decided it would be nice to retire to the hot tub in the lobby of the hotel. Lyla was loving the handsome stranger's company. She found him most interesting and completely fun to be with. He made her laugh.
She needed that badly, but she had to say,

"Sorry, can't do. If you had told me before I came, I could have brought along a bathing suit!"
William laughed and said,

"Oh, yea of little faith! Where there is a will, there is a way!"

With that statement William walked over to the registering counter and had a talk with the man behind the desk. Lyla could tell that the man behind the desk was disagreeing with her handsome stranger to begin with. She saw the clerk shake his head (No). She could not help but wonder what this persuasive man was trying to accomplish by badgering this poor smaller, bald

47

headed desk clerk. Watching through the large glass windows, suddenly she felt weak and fearful when she realized quickly that this man most likely always got exactly what he wanted out of life. In less than two minutes, as she sat there in wonderment, she noticed the man behind the counter walk across the lobby with a large ring of keys in his hands. As the two men passed the door of the restaurant, William stuck his head into the doorway. He seemed to not notice or even care that other people were in the restaurant when she heard him say loudly,

"Lyla, what size do you wear?"
She was embarrassed as she told him her size, but she was also very amazed. William had persuaded the poor desk clerk to open the closed gift shop long enough for him to purchase her a bathing suit. She was shocked at the power this man controlled.

Within a few minutes the handsome stranger walked back into the restaurant with a bag in his hand. Lyla looked inside to find a pretty black bathing suit and a colorful towel. She was surprised at this man's good taste and extremely surprised at his actions. Lyla was finding out that this man amazed her completely in seemingly every way. She was not sure she had ever met anyone quite like this man. She also was not sure whether that was a good thing or a bad thing!

While sitting back down and acting as though what had just happened was a normal day's occurrence, William motioned for the waiter to bring them still another bottle of the very special wine. This time he ask for two glasses and he said,

"Put that on my tab."

Lyla noticed how everyone in this hotel seemed to know this man by name and watched as the waiter said,

"Yes Sir Mr. Jenson! I'll do that very thing!"

With that, William pulled out Lyla's chair. She lifted herself up from her seating position only to notice how short she seemed to be with this handsome man. She had worn lower shoes than usual tonight and she felt sheltered over by this massive man. Being close to five-foot eight, Lyla could hardly remember ever being around a man that she had to look up to other than some members of her own family. Tonight she somehow felt small and yielding. This was a most strange place to be for the strong Miss Lyla Jane Wilson! Yet she followed along behind this masterful man like a little puppy dog until they got to the hot tub. He pointed to a bathroom and told her to go there to change, but then added with a twinkle in his eyes,

"Unless of course; you would rather go to my room to change! Then maybe we might just forget spending any time in that hot tub." Lyla shivered. Was she ready for all of this? Would she be able to keep control over herself with this man? Would she be in danger of losing all of her self-respect? Somehow she knew that she was like putty or clay in this man's hands. A more focused or powerful man she knew she had never met. What was she to do? Run? That would probably be the wise thing to do. Maybe it was just the wine, but Lyla was now losing much of the comfort zone feeling that she had felt earlier. She was now starting to question what she was doing there.

As if William could read every thought she had, he said,

"Lyla, I am not a dangerous man! I will take it slow! I find you very attractive and I am finding that I am enjoying being with you entirely too much for my own wellbeing. Maybe I should be the one to raise my eyebrow and think about running!"

With that they both laughed and Lyla left for the bathroom to change her clothing. William had said he would run to his room and change his clothing and be back momentarily.

Lyla looked at herself in the mirror. Yes, she realized that she was pretty. It took her years to get that much self-esteem, but finally she had realized that she was probably a beautiful woman. She also knew that the man she was spending the evening with was most probably one of the most handsome men she had ever laid eyes upon. She, of course, knew there was so much more to a person than that.

Lyla hated herself for analyzing every situation to pieces. She did know that very handsome men usually expected and usually got everything and anything that they ever wanted. She knew that she could not let herself fall into any traps. She could tell that William T. Jenson's looks and size probably made his life easier while requesting what he wanted, just the same as her looks had always gotten her foot into a door. But, she also knew from spending the evening with this man that he was most likely not that shallow. He did have depth and she hoped that he too knew there was much more to a person than their good looks.

William was either very fast, or his room was next to the hot tub, because he was already settled down into the steaming water when Lyla walked out of the bathroom. As she walked across the floor she could feel the steam of William's eyes watch every step that she took. She was so relieved to take each step deeper into the water. Finally when the water covered her nakedness, William handed her a glass of wine. Her nerves were about to settle when he said,

"Say lady! Do you know you have a beautiful body?"
Then he added a verse to an old song in his joking and jolly way,

"If I told you that you had a beautiful body, would you hold it against me?"
Both laughed. Okay, now Lyla was nervous. This was a grown up game they were playing and yes this was more than likely only a sexual encounter. Could she handle this? She had told herself over and over again that, yes, yes, she could. She knew that she did not want another long commented relationship, *so*, why not? Why not just have some fun like so many do in the rest of the world? Why was she so uptight anyway? She knew that the rest of the world was so much more relaxed than she. Others were comfortable while having just pure sexual encounters occasionally. Why did she always have to think in terms of relationships? Why was she so rigid? Then she thought of how maybe the wine would loosen her up a bit. God knows she had had enough of that this evening.

As the evening passed, not once did William put his hands upon Lyla. This was to her surprise! He had gotten her into a bathing suit. He had filled her with enough wine to where she knew that she was very mellow. However, the conversation was lovely and the companionship was wonderful. After about an hour, William told Lyla that he was not going to offer her another glass of wine because he knew that she would need to drive home. Then jokingly said,

"Unless, of course; you would like to spend the night with me!"
With this remark, Lyla was feeling very comfortable. She had learned enough about her handsome stranger now to know that he was only teasing. This was something he liked to do and Lyla found it most refreshing.

The couple stayed in the hot tub until the wee hours of the morning. They were talking, laughing and getting acquainted. Finally Lyla excused herself with the statement that both of them had to go to work the following morning. She thanked her stranger for a wonderful evening and walked to the restroom to change. When she came back out of the restroom she knew that she most surely looked terrible in the bright lights of the hall. She had steamed off all of her makeup and she had drank enough wine to where it showed in her eyes. She was embarrassed when she found William waiting for her at the door of the bathroom. He was dressed and he told her that he would walk her to her car. This was a good idea and she wondered why she had not thought about that herself at this late hour.

As they arrived at the door of Lyla's car, William reached over and took Lyla into his arms. He said,

"You know you are beautiful, don't you? I want you to know I enjoyed this evening more than I have enjoyed any evening for a very long time."

He reached around and stuck a card into Lyla's open purse. Then he said,

"Here is my number! When you get home, please call me so I will not worry!"

There was that comfort zone again. The zone that made Lyla feel like they were married. Lyla said,

"Okay and Thank You!"

William placed a wonderful kiss upon her lips. She was not expecting that either, but she melted into his arms just the same. She was thinking,

"I could get used to this!"

As the strong man let loose of his grip upon her, she looked up to see the handsome face under that large brimmed hat. She felt as if it was a protective roof over her head and she felt very, very small. Yet, she felt very safe in this big man's arms.

C hapter 4

During the years alone and after Lyla's husband had died, she had been having many deep feelings on many subjects. She had lived alone for more than a few years and many people may have believed her to have become eccentric. Many dreams or visions had come to her after her husband's death. She felt she had seen him on different occasions. She even felt she had spoken with him one night. Rarely did she tell anyone except maybe some to her children. Telling these stories had been Lyla's downfall. She knew that her children now believed her to be completely insane.

Lyla's children had worried about her while she was still living in the marriage home. Then they worried about their mother when she migrated to the north. She knew that these dreams had been a big factor in her move home. The children were one-hundred percent on board about her move. Actually they had insisted that she move to her home land of Nevada in the Western United States, hoping to put their mother in familiar territory. This was where the children believed that she could have a large support group of her other family members. They believed this is where she would be able to better deal with her grief. They felt she was only delaying the sadness by moving to other areas. They believed she was running from her pain and loneliness. This was probably very true.

Yet, Lyla felt too many questions had gone unanswered. Maybe she *was* losing her mind? If so, at least that would be a good explanation for the recurring dream that she was now having on a regular basis. She could maybe live with the thought that she was crazy. Sadly, even crazy could never explain what she saw or how she felt about those houses in Louisiana. Those houses and those living in them kept coming into her dreams. They were far too genuine to be anything but real. Spooky as that may seem! There was no explanation for the facts about those houses short of paranormal!

Lyla shook herself. One would think that after a wonderful encounter with a beautiful man such as the one she just had; all dreams of disturbing things would have gone away. But no! Those houses and that little girl just kept coming back to her. She had thought earlier that these dreams may have come about because of her loneliness. But, now she was very happy. She had met a handsome stranger. She was getting more and more acquainted with him with each passing day. She certainly liked what she was seeing. If these dreams were some kind of a crutch, well then she needed them no longer.

No matter how hard Lyla tried to talk herself out of the facts of the dreams, she could not shake them. Instead of going away, the dreams seemed to be ever more constant lately. The realization of that the house with the cold rocks where she knew that her seven year old bare feet had touched kept coming back even during the times she was spending with her handsome stranger. Then there was the realization that the long old house was not even visible from the road; being only visible if one got out of the car and took a walk. This fact kept Lyla dumbfounded. In one of her dreams, she realized the little girl's name must be Flossy Mae, even though she knew it was herself. Crazy as that may sound. In one dream Lyla could hear someone holler for Flossy Mae and she answered. These things left too many questions unanswered. These things had her believing that maybe she was in fact going crazy.

At this time, Lyla knew she might be ready for a new relationship in so many ways. She was not fond of being alone. Yet, she knew that this was the safest way to live to protect her heart from more pain and this is what she had chosen for herself. However, the new handsome stranger was making her want a relationship with a man. She did not realize how much she had missed that closeness. She also believed that she may have to resolve many of her problems before that could happen. She had really been fascinated by this new southern gentleman. She felt he may be sincere, even though she could not help but notice he was one *Hell of a Flirt*!

Lyla would talk herself down with the fact that this man traveled all of the time and he most probably had a woman at every port. For all that she knew, this man could even be married. She had not seen a wedding ring, but he could have put it in a pocket or something. There were so many tricks one could play on another. She also knew that she did not just get off the boat. She had probably had things tried on her or had heard of about every trickery in the book. Yet, there seemed to be a deep connection between the two of them that she could not explain. There was closeness or a good feeling of being home when she was with this man. As she tossed her thoughts around in her head, she realized the jury was still out on this one. She laughed at herself and said,

"The jury had better stay out for a good long time on this one, Ole' girl!"

All Lyla knew for certain was that she needed to learn how to best resolve any issues that she may have before ever starting any kind of a relationship. So far the southern gentleman and she had only had dinners. He stayed almost a week and she had eaten with him each and every evening of his stay. He was off to another adventure by now and probably many states away. She may never hear from him again. That would be a shame, but she knew that that would be okay too. Before meeting William, other than her dreams, she had seemed to be in a rut with her life.

A week passed and Lyla had proceeded to work on one goal. That goal was to find out more about herself. She had surprised herself on how easily it was for William to walk into her life and upset all of her settled plans in the way that he did. She knew that she was a bit aggravated with herself for being taken in. She knew that she felt this way because he had not called in this week and she would be danged if she would call him. That is probably what he expected. She had a feeling that the great Mr. William T. Jenson was so ate up with himself to where he may believe that he was irresistible to the opposite sex. Whether that is what he thought or not, he must be irresistible, because he *had* caused her way of thinking to go in a totally different direction than she had ever planned. With all of these thoughts racing through her head, she knew that she was just disgusted with herself for being so weak. Yet, if William was the type of man she was now trying to make him out to be, why had he not tried to have sex with her?

Lyla knew that even if she never seen William again, if she could be that easily persuaded, what was to keep her from ending up with another husband. What was to keep her from moving around somewhere and messing up her life? So as of now, she was on a crusade to find out more about Lyla!

Another factor or factors messing up Lyla's way of thinking, were those continuing dreams! She had to know as to why she would have such dreams. Often she would have the same one over and over again! She had to find out why she would have had the experience that she had in Louisiana. Going to a shrink could not help. There was just too much there for them to explain away. She doubted very much that she was having these dreams because she hated her mother or something silly like that. She laughed at herself for thinking that way. Besides, she adored her mother. Doctors would most likely medicate her, write her out a bill as long as her arm, and then tell her to be on her way!

Lyla did know that her dreams had to be explained and resolved in some way! Otherwise, she could be very sure that the dreams would surely cause her to go insane? She would try to console herself and try to find answers to her questions as to why she had found that house in the first place. Why her? Why or how could a couple of old broken down houses mess with one's mind as these were doing to her. She now made it her life's ambition to find the answers to her questions. She figured she must plan another trip to Louisiana. Then again, would that help or would it make it all worse?

On this quest of looking for answers, Lyla started to wonder if maybe she was a descendant of the plantation owner. Then she thought,

"What would that have to do with it?"
She tried to radicalize everything. One thing she could not understand was that her dreams were leading her in a direction that was trying to make her think that she was most possibly, or likely she was Miss Flossy Mae. Maybe this person was a spirit trying to tell the world something through her, if someone could believe in such a thing.
Then she would think,

"No, that cannot be it. I was that seven year old child. I was standing there barefooted. I know it was me!"

In order for that to be true, one would have to believe in reincarnation. Lyla knew most that she did not! While thrashing through all of these ideas, Lyla realized that she was most properly the wrong color to be related to Miss Flossy Mae. Something had told her that Flossy Mae was a black child. Many, Many thoughts crossed her mind.

A friend to whom Lyla had finally confined in told her that she needed to check out hypnosis or she needed to talk with some Shamans or something like that. Lyla knew this to be true. She knew that she must go to someone with an open mind. She was embarrassed and she was very sure she did not want to talk to anyone who would laugh at her thoughts. She knew her friend to be right. That would be the best avenue to take. She had better go to someone who knew of experiences with reincarnation, ghost haunting or that of channeling. She was maybe being haunted.

When Lyla would think of these things she would chew herself out. She did not believe in such things! She was a professional business woman who had always been so matter of fact in every way. She was educated. She was religious. She was rational. How silly could she be now in her middle age? Yet, she knew that there must be someone trying to get through to her even with all of her doubts. It was stronger than she! She knew this because she had put up one Hell of a fight in disbelief! Yet, this entity still came through loud and clear in her dreams and her visions!

The reason Lyla had confined in her friend was because she was an Indian and African American descendant. Her friend was a deep, deep person and Lyla loved her dearly. This friend had once served on a board for a company Lyla had worked for. She was a pillar of strength through many petty grievances that so many of the power stricken board members tried to place upon their employees. This sweet lady was always a wonderful friend to Lyla. She remained a loyal board member but did not agree with one side of the situations or the other. She never once attacked her friend Lyla. For these and many other reasons, Lyla would also remain devoted to this lovely lady.

After not seeing her friend for many, many years and not staying in contact; Lyla had called her to ask for her help. She realized that she was horrible about staying in contact with those she cared the most about. But thankfully even those kinds of things were changing now of days, thanks to the computer world. A few weeks ago she had heard from a friend she had not seen since high school. This was such a thrill for Lyla. She did not mean to be so distant. There were many, many individuals that she cared a great deal about. Life just always seemed to get in her way.

After all of the excitement of catching up, and taking all of her good friends well guided advice to heart, Lyla asked her friend about her sister. She knew that this sister was a Shaman type and could possibly shed some light on her situation. The sister had once placed her hands upon Lyla at a party that was held at an art galleria and had told her things that really hit home. The sister had noticed Lyla favoring her left shoulder. She had asked if her shoulder hurt. Lyla had answered her questioning with,

"Yes, my shoulder hurts!"

The sister then, while making friendly conversation, asked if Lyla was married. This was shortly after the death of her husband, so she answered with a quiet,

"I'm widowed!"

Thinking that would satisfy any questions. But the sister probed on with,

"What did your husband die from?"

Lyla answered,

"His heart!"

The sister then started shaking her head as if she had already known the answer. She remarked that this was the reason for the shoulder ache. The left shoulder would hurt with your heart and due to the recent death of her other half, she was feeling his pain.

Lyla became very fascinated with this woman and continued to speak with her. Before the evening was over, the friend's sister had told Lyla that she had lived many lives. She had told her that she was a very old soul. Lyla somehow knew that fact already, even though all of this kind of stuff was totally against anything she had been raised to believe. Lyla felt this was all very true. She had never in her life felt like a child. She was always very serious minded. She could barely remember playing with anything. From childhood she had always had dreams of places she had never been or of people she had never met.

At one family reunion an uncle was showing some really old pictures. He pointed out that Lyla was the total image of her great, great grandmother. Lyla looked at the picture and realized the picture looked as if it were her, but dressed in the 1800's clothing. The strange thing about that was that Lyla had had dreams of that very same house in which the grandmother was on the front porch. Lyla was young at the time of that reunion and had never thought much more about it. She had every right to look just as her grandmother had looked. Family looks do that. So, that occurrence was brushed aside and far, far from her mind.

While talking with her friend's sister that night; the thoughts of that reunion day returned. Lyla wondered if she actually could be her great-great grandmother reincarnated. Lyla tried to keep an open mind about everything. She believed as others, but she often believed religious beliefs passed down generation after generation may put clouds over people's eyes by not letting them see the whole picture. However, these kinds of thoughts always made her feel sinful, so she would quickly erase them from her mind.

The meeting with this sister at that party during the past years was after the last road trip through Louisiana but before the, oh so vivid imagines Lyla was feeling now. That conversation was more of a cocktail party conversation and at the time Lyla had not put much value upon what was said. Now, she was not so sure. Maybe everything her wonderful friend's sister had said was true. She had noticed the dark eyes of this sister staring ever so deeply inside of her soul. She could feel her presence so vividly. After one period of looking into her soul for what seemed like forever, the lady had told Lyla that she had lived so many lives by now to where she would not have to come back after this life if she so chose. Lyla had dismissed everything that was said, but now it was all coming back to her. She must talk with her friend's sister. It was so very important! She knew that this was most probably the only person on earth who could help her now!

During the phone conversation, Lyla learned that the sister had gone back to Alaska where she had lived for all of her adult years. The time she had met her, she was only visiting with Lyla's friend and her mother. This did not matter. Lyla had to talk with her. This was of most importance by now for Lyla's sanity. She asked her friend to please ask her sister if she could come visit her. Lyla had been in every other state except Alaska and told herself if nothing else came out of the visit, at least she would have accomplished visiting every state in the United States. Thankfully the good friend had said she would fulfill Lyla's request.

By now to Lyla's surprise, William had called often. Each week she and the handsome stranger were becoming more and more acquainted by phone. She was finding herself waiting impatiently when she knew he would call. She had even called a few times herself by this date. There was something very mysterious about Mr. William T. Jenson she would think. He was mysterious, exciting, comforting, and troubling all wrapped up into one package. She did not truthfully know how to describe this handsome, sexy, wonderful man.

Lyla also knew there would never be a way to explain her dreams nor the trip she was hoping for to Alaska to Mr. William T. Jenson, so she knew most she would have to make up something. Her relationship with William was far too new for him to get questions in his mind as to whether she was crazy or not.

A few weeks passed and Lyla got the phone call that she had so desperately waited on. Her good friend called with a phone number, an address and a date that would be appropriate for a visit to Alaska. She was going to the sister's home. This could be very exciting. Lyla called the sister and was so relieved to have an appointment. She put down the phone and made flight and travel arrangements immediately. This was to be an exciting trip and Lyla was hoping it would be most beneficial.

In the month of July, Lyla was on her way to Alaska. Thoughts kept going through her mind as to whether she was being silly or not. Then she would just as suddenly realize that this was not silly. There was absolutely no explanation for her experiences short of paranormal. She had to find out the truth. At least speaking with her good friend's sister, she would be in a comfort zone. She would be speaking to someone kind and someone she found to be quite friendly. This woman would never make her feel stupid about her dreams.

When Lyla arrived at the Anchorage Airport, she was greeted by Tywanda. This lady was about the same age as Lyla and had long black hair that she wore in a thick long braid hanging way down her back, just the same as her sister Ina. The black eyes were just as dark as Lyla had remembered. Those eyes could look straight through a person. Yet, one could feel the warmth and the kindness exert from every glance.

Tywanda remarked,

"Gee, it is good to see someone from the lower forty-eight. I do see many often, but no one that I know, so it is wonderful to have you. I hope you enjoy your visit."

Lilia told the lady that she had booked a room at the Marriot and would like to freshen up and then take Tywanda out to dinner if she so desired. Lyla remembered the friend saying that her sister lived some ways from town. Tywanda thought the dinner idea was wonderful, so the two picked up the luggage and headed for the Marriot. Tywanda knew of a nice seafood restaurant that carried Alaskan crab legs and lobster. The wonderful way that she described the place, Lyla could not wait to go.

In a while the women walked into the darkened restaurant and a maître d' seated the two in a dark corner booth. Lyla was comforted by this jester because she felt she could speak more freely when she knew no one else would be listening. Her predicament had become quite embarrassing by this date. She rarely told anyone and if she did let anything slip, she would make some sort of a joke out of it.

Once seated, choices were made from the menu and the drinks were ordered. Tywanda took Lyla's hands into hers. She sat there for the longest time while holding her hands. Lyla did not feel uncomfortable as one would think. Actually she felt the total opposite. The Shaman's hand touching was rather soothing. Lyla began to relax.

As if coming back from a trace, Tywanda started to speak. She said,

"Lyla, you have been through so very much! I have to tell you that history often repeats itself."

She did not remember telling Lyla years ago that she had lived many lives, so once again she said,

"You have lived so many lives!"

And then as her voice was fading out into the distance, she said,

"So, so many tragic lives!"

Lyla somehow knew this, but it was so good to hear it from someone else.

The waiter approached the table with the drinks. Lyla noticed how the walls of this restaurant were covered with swordfish and many kinds of sea fish that she had never seen. She was in the deep sea, heavy fishing belt right now. She was so anticipating the wonderful meal she knew she was about to receive. She loved seafood; especially if it was fresh. She had eaten very little on the plane, so she was very hungry now.

As Lyla's thoughts came back to the matter at hand, she asked the Shaman Tywanda if she believed that she could have been mixed with African blood. Tywanda laughed at her and said,

"If so, it surely does not show, you are probably the lightest and the blondest person I have ever met."
The women both had a good laugh. Then Tywanda said,

"I am sure that is possible. As many years as we have been mixing, I often wonder if there are any true African or true Europeans' in our country. You have gotten my curiosity up though. Why do you ask?"
Lyla answered with,

"The story I am about to tell you is going to be very hard for you to believe. This will blow your mind! I am *NOW* almost positive that I was once a black slave girl!"
The Shaman glared deeply into Lyla's eyes. Her deep black eyes were burning a hole through her it seemed. One could tell that she thought with very deep thoughts. She never made light of Lyla for what she had just said. She did not come back with something like,

"Sorry, you are crazy! I cannot help you!"
This was what Lyla had feared the most. Suddenly the Shaman Tywanda looked at her with eyes that got even darker when she said,

"Lyla, you do not have to be black, white, red or yellow. You do not have to be any certain color in a reincarnation. It is a human condition. One can come back in any color or in any nation. You are not necessarily a reincarnation of any of your family members or of your own race."

Then, while the Shaman seemed to be in deep thought, she added,

"However, you were your great, great grandmother!"

Lyla's mouth fell open! She now remembered her uncle's remarks from thirty years ago. My, My! It was true. Now, Lyla knew this woman was one-hundred percent what she claimed to be. She was surely going to be able to explain everything. Thank God, she had made the correct journey!

Dinner was delicious! Tywanda suggested the two retire to a lounging section in the bar area of the restaurant. Lyla was impressed with the large leather covered couches that sat in group seating all along the walls. Thankfully the place did not seem to be overly crowded tonight. The ladies could have a nice comfortable conversation.

While Lyla was taking in her surroundings and ordering a glass of HMV Chardonnay; she could not help but notice this was truly the United States. The wine was her very favorite wine from California and the waiter did not bat an eye while completing her request. Why then, did she feel as though she was a million miles away from her homeland? She had been to Canada, England, Bermuda and many other English speaking countries. All of those places had made her feel completely at home. She always thought that was because most everyone could speak English. Well, Alaskans spoke English! It must be the terrain and the unusual flowers that made her feel as though she was in a distant and strange foreign country.

As Lyla was getting more comfortable, she realized she had overdressed. She had believed Alaska to be a place she would surely freeze to death while there. She had packed only heavy clothing. Right now, with the pretty fire place burning in shades of red and yellow, her heavy woven turtleneck sweater was becoming a bit much. What could she do now but suffer through it. She moved closer to the edge of the couch. When Tywanda noticed the problem she asked the waiter if they could take their drinks and move to another seating. They all agreed and the much cooler section of the room was much more suitable.

Tywanda began the conversation by asking,

"Tell me Lyla, what has been troubling you so terribly much. Is it the slave girl? I heard you are questioning reincarnation. My sister is very fond of you and she told me she is worried about you. She said that all of this has you extremely stressed. Is it the awareness that you have lived before?"

Lyla was not really sure of how to answer that question. She only wanted to keep an open mind at this point. She knew something had happened to her that was so strong and so very unusual. She also knew that her church taught that it was appointed unto man once to die. Most believed that this passage would mean there was only one life per person. Yet the words of the Bible had also said that one would live forever.

She wondered if this could be interpreted as a reincarnation type of living. If one were born again and again and again, that would mean that one would live forever. Those thoughts only made her think that she was being un-religious and she would hang her head and become ashamed.

Lyla started telling the Shaman of the dreams she had been having since just a child. She had never understood any of those dreams, but she was wise enough to realize that many of the so called dreams were more than just dreams. These dreams were just too very real. She told of how in one dream she found herself in a crowded room. The room was shadow lighted and very dark. She remembered a large group of people fitting ever so tightly into this room. They were pressing up against each other. She told of how she felt she knew every one of these people and she felt they were all very close. She could hear their thoughts. They somehow felt like a part of her. The Shaman Tywanda's face lit up when she said,

"Girl, do I ever want to talk to you! You do not realize it, but you have a wonderful miracle gift. This is a very special gift. A very, very special gift indeed! Most everyone in this world of ours will never have the experiences you are telling me about."

Her eyes got large with much excitement when she said,

"**Do you know what that dream meant?**"
Lyla said,

"No!"
Tywanda said,

"In your dream you were seeing all of your lives at one time. All of those people were **you**. If you walk into another room looking the same, but filled with more people, they are your **soul mate**!

The soul mate would have also lived many lives the same as you and with you. That room was filled with your people over thousands of years. It does, however feel to me that you skip ever so many generations. I don't know why, unless that is of your choosing. While I was reading your enter voices a while ago, I did not get the idea that you had any lives between your great, great grandmother and you now. The only vibe I did get to dispute that theory was a large three story white house. There is an embankment behind it and something is wrong on the third floor. Lyla gasped!

"Oh, my God, I have dreamed that dream over and over again. I dream of a house with a normal porch on the front. This house may have been built at about the turn of the century or early 1900's. It is a pretty house in a town or a city. It has a nice small yard that is flat with the sidewalk until you go to the backyard. Then there is not much of a yard at all. It has a wall or a hill of sorts that cuts the yard off completely. There is however, a lot of yellow flowers at the base of that wall. As for the third floor, I am somehow scared to death of that floor. I will not go near it. Yet I look up at it all of the time. There is a shadowy yellow light coming from that third floor, but I never enter it. I have such a large fear of that floor."

Tywanda said,

"Exactly! Now I feel this was a very brief life for you. After hearing your dream, I realize you did have another life between the two mentioned. I believe the only part of that life was lived in that house. I do believe that you lived very shortly in that life. The reason for that belief is because I cannot get any readings at all from it other than the house and the yard."

Lyla was satisfied with the answer because that would put one tortured dream to rest. Tywanda prompted her to continue with her stories. It was so wonderful to finally be able to tell someone everything, while knowing there would be no harsh judgment placed upon her.

As Lyla began telling about the Louisiana trips, Tywanda was in a very deep thought. She was listening intensely, but she was also staring deeply into Lyla's very soul. It was strange that Lyla could feel an energy coming from within her and going into Tywanda. She explained why these dreams or visions had disturbed her so very much. She told of how they had to be much more than just a dream. She told that she believed this because there was no way that she could have seen that old shack house before getting out of her car and walking over to the embankment! Finally Lyla felt she had told the whole story! She had explained that these experiences were what had been troubling her so badly lately. She then said,

"That is all I remember!"

Tywanda was very silent for a while and then she spoke in a polite, bedside style manner of voice and said,

"Lyla, you have to let Flossy Mae in! Open up your heart and let her come into your dreams. You have shut her out for way too long. She has been trying to come through for generation after generation. She has so many unresolved issues. She is haunting you because she wants you to know something important. There is some reason

73

she wishes to contact you. She could even be trying to warn you about something. I felt her a while ago and I believe she is here to either warn you or to set something straight. She wants you to be aware of something. I have no idea of what that is. She cannot tell me. You have to let her in. She tries to protect you. I feel that she has tried to protect you in every life since hers. You rarely let her in. If you do, the time you give is too brief for her to explain. Your strongest block of her was when the time was a more Victorian time and your belief system was so strong to where you would not give her any chance to explain. Feeling her vibes as I do, I realize that she wants you to know she is sorry for your sadness, but that she is very proud of what you have done with this life. Then it was as if I heard her say, 'Our life'!"

Lyla was shocked. She was Flossy Mae reincarnated. Tywanda explained of how Flossy Mae probably felt that Lyla was a more open minded individual in the early 2000's than she would have ever been back in another life. Tywanda also estimated that it was possible that the life that Flossy Mae was speaking of was more than likely the short life she had lived in that Victorian home. Tywanda now had a feeling the person living Lyla's life at that time was possibly murdered. Maybe even on that third floor.

The comfort zone that the Shaman Tywanda had given Lyla made her think of many other dreams. She remembered one that she could not understand. This dream was as if she were living in a group home of sorts, or maybe a boarding house.   She can see braided, woven rugs throughout the halls that are leading to many, many rooms.   These rugs seem dusty and dirty. She sees many beds and old brown covered comforters.   She felt that at one time a group of women were placed in an attic and were standing naked in a row out from a tapered ceiling so as not to bump their heads.   This attic was of only wood, no decorations or furniture of any kind.   She felt that this line of women had been formed so a group of men could choose which woman they wanted.   Lyla knew that she felt dirty and useless in this dream.   Since she was starting to believe that it was possible that she had lived many different lives, she was now wondering if maybe she had been sold into white slavery, or possibly she was a prostitute in the 1700's, 1800's or the early 1900's.

Lyla expected Tywanda to laugh at this dream, but she did not. Instead she said,

"Lyla, with the gift you have, there are others who are trying to right a wrong done to them. They will sometimes try to come through to you when they cannot get their later selves to accept them. I do not believe you lived that life. I do however; feel the modern person who did live that life is completely shut down to any possibilities. The person she is now in the 2000's will not let a pervious person in. You are a channel and many may have wished to use you. You will definitely know when a pervious person comes through to you and it was actually you. Can you tell the difference now?"

Lyla thought for a minute, then said,

"Yes! The dream I just told you about was only one time. It was while I was still a child and it was not as intense. I think I am beginning to understand. When it is actually me, I have that dream over and over again. I also feel I am actually living each step of that person's life. I am not just seeing myself standing naked in front of a bunch of men as I did in that dream. As I remember, it seemed that I was standing a distance in front of this girl while watching what was happening. In my dreams when it is really me, I am in that body. I am standing on those cold rocks. I am touching the items. I am living that life. Yes, I can definitely tell the difference!"

Lyla seemed pleased with herself for making that distinction. Tywanda talked some more about how to accept the dreams and the visions. She assured Lyla that she would not loose herself as she had feared. She would not go insane. She needed to accept the dreams as part of her life and learn the lessons told to her. Obviously, Flossy Mae had a very important story to tell Lyla and she had best listen. Tywanda told her it may be important enough to mean life or death. She said,

"This lovely lady did not travel through time to only check up on you. She has something *very* important to tell you."

The long evening came to an end. It had been so revealing and so liberating to where Lyla hated for this visit to end. She had booked a fight back to the lower forty-eight for that next morning. So, she said her goodbyes to the lovely lady named Tywanda and headed for her room. That night she slept better than she had in years. There were no dreams, but she was most comfortable and cozy. The flight back was just as enjoyable.

Lyla felt as if a large rock had been removed from off her very being. She now understood and she would try to understand more. She could now live with her knowledge and be grateful for it. She was determined to get to know Flossy Mae better. Suddenly she felt honored to have been given such a gift! She was no longer afraid. She was going to accept and be open to anything that Flossy Mae wished to tell her or wished for her to see. But, she knew she could not force the issue. She knew Flossy Mae had to come to her in her own good time. The next time she would be ready with an open mind and welcome her with open arms.

Chapter 5

Lyla arrived home safely and started back to work. She worked for several months without much worry over her trip or conversations. A new settling piece or calmness had come over this lovely woman. Even though Lyla had believed her encounter with the handsome William T. Jenson was a fleeting one time deal, she was happy to find this not to be the case. Her handsome southern gentleman had returned for several visits during his travels through the pretty State of Nevada. He always phoned Lyla. They always had a nice dinner and lots of fun together. Lyla had learned that this man had a childish side to him and she often laughed at him while he would spend hours playing a child's game on a store's slot machine. It warmed Lyla's heart to watch this huge man melt into a giggling ten year old when a game would end as he hoped. It was great fun to be with this man. She awaited his return each time with great anticipation!

Christmas came with Lyla visiting her son and his family in Texas. The trip was wonderful. Lyla took her mother. Her daughter and granddaughter joined them by means of flight. The only disappointment was that the youngest son could not join them this year. Some of the family traveled back by car to their home state together. The daughter and her family would be visiting her mother and grandmother a while longer. Fun was had by all and it was such a wonderful blessing for Lyla to see this group of children and grandchildren all together. She was saddened by the fact that she had other loved ones that she

would not be able to see this year. Everything in Lyla's life seemed to have to be some sort of a tradeoff and she did not like that one bit. When her daughter's visit came to an end, she was saddened, but she had a few days off between Christmas and New Year's. She decided to enjoy those days by visiting with her mother. Her mother was getting elderly and she most usually took a nap each afternoon. This was not strange considering the woman stayed up really late and would always be up before daylight.
Short naps obviously became a necessity.

Lyla's mother lived in the mountain part of the state. One day it was snowing. No one could go anywhere. The snow was coming down so fast to where it would have been useless to run snowplows. The highway department had decided to wait until the blizzard was over before attempting any kind of a cleanup.

Lyla's mother did not have cable TV. It was something she had never had a desire to have. Today, nothing seemed to be on the few channels of her TV that she did have. So, Lyla had found a book and was reading it while her mother was asleep. Before long, Lyla was asleep as well. A cold winter day at one's mothers, all snuggled up in a wool blanket in front of a fireplace that is sending out its warmth, what more could one ask for than to become completely comfortable. Lyla did just that. In her twilight vision she was aware of the fireplace and aware that she was at her mothers. This comfort zone was the best place in the entire world to be. She was enjoying her visit with much delight.

Finally, Lyla was in a deep afternoon sleep. The snow kept coming down and the house was darkened by the weather. It had been months since she had any strange dreams. Oh, she might have had a fleeting dream about something that had happened that day and so on, but there were none of those vision type dreams. She somehow felt disappointed. She started thinking that maybe she had displeased Flossy Mae by her non-belief in the beginning to where she would not come to her again. Then she thought,

"Flossy Mae is me! Why can't I just bring her back whenever I want?"
This must have triggered something in Lyla's mind because she had a dream that very afternoon. It was a short dream, but it was of Flossy Mae. In this dream Flossy Mae was an adult. She was cleaning up a beautiful old fashioned kitchen. She had a bandana wrapped around her head in a turban style. She was singing an old hymn.

Lyla was awakened when her mother awoke. Her mother had something that needed done in another room so she left Lyla briefly in her comfort zone. She felt so relaxed at this time. In this mode she started analyzing the dream. This was highly unusual with her dreams of Flossy Mae. The dreams most usually drained her out like an old wash rag. She had started to tell her mother about her dream but thought better of that. Her mother was of a strong religious faith and would shame her, pray for her and then worry about her.

Lyla was so satisfied with the dream this time because she was always inside of Flossy Mae's body. She was Flossy Mae! The problem

81

with that was that she had no idea what Flossy Mae looked like. She could feel everything that Flossy Mae felt, but she could not see what she looked like in the face. In this short dream, Flossy Mae was a young woman. She had straightened her headdress in a small mirror that was hanging close to a cook stove. Lyla was so very pleased. She saw a truly beautiful black woman looking back at her. The young woman had sharp facial features that were not that unlike her own. She had a sharp nose and high cheek bones. She was very, very attractive. Lyla only had a problem with her color. It seemed so unusual looking into a mirror and seeing a black woman looking back at her. She knew one thing from this experience though, and that was that color definitely does not matter. You feel exactly the same on the inside.

Lyla enjoyed the rest of the week with her mother, but had to return home once the roads were cleared. Her time off from work was coming to an end. Two nights after her arrival at her own place, she had another dream or vision of Flossy Mae. This one was a most terrifying dream. This was on a Tuesday night. It was so terrifying to where Lyla woke up screaming.

Somewhere in the night, Lyla saw herself and several other people hiding in tall weeds. She was up against a wood fence. This fence was a kind she had only seen in Virginia. A split wood fencing that crisscrossed each board while forming triangles. The length of the boards in one section of the fence would go one way, then the boards in another section of the fence would go the other way, causing a 'V' shaped space in each section. Flossy Mae and the people she was with were scattered between two or three of these sections. They were hunkered down in the tall weeds. Someone was shooting at them. Men on horses were riding up and shooting at Flossy Mae and the other people. Suddenly she somehow knew that the other people were none other than her own children. Total fear overcame Lyla and she awakened screaming! She went to the kitchen and fixed herself a cup of hot tea. She turned on the TV and tried to get her mind off of whatever just happened. She knew that the Shaman had told her not to shut out Flossy Mae in anyway, but fear was keeping her from wanting to go back to sleep. Finally she turned off the TV, drank her tea and tried to analyze that terrifying dream. No, that was a vision! She knew beyond a shadow of a doubt that none of these experiences could be considered to be a dream! To go to sleep meant she had to live through whatever Flossy Mae had lived through. She was so feared!

Finally Lyla realized she must finish that dream. She tried to think, probably a safety inside of her trying not to go to sleep. She thought of how the fencing was only done of old. This was a type of fence used by farmers or plantation owners before modern conveniences. This, she knew definitely had to be one of Flossy Mae's experiences. She knew Flossy Mae had lived this terrifying night, just as she was living it all over again this night. All of a sudden it really hit her! She realized that, yes Flossy Mae must have something extremely important to warn her about. Why else would she put herself through these horrible nightmares again? Her life was long over.

Her tribulations were no more. Why would she let herself ever live it over again? Of course she knew once again that Flossy Mae was also herself, so it may be her period person who wanted to know all of this. With that, Lyla started to talk with Flossy Mae. She asked,

"Is that you Flossy Mae? Or me!"
She laughed while she was thinking of how very strange this whole experience seemed to be.

After about an hour, Lyla realized she should not be afraid and headed back for the bedroom. She fell asleep immediately only to get right back into that dream. This time she was sure it was Flossy Mae and her children. The whole family was scrunched down in the tall weeds. They hovered close to the split wood fence. There was a group of men on horseback coming towards them. Somehow Lyla knew this was a group of Slave Patrolmen and they were getting ever closer. All of a sudden, Lyla could feel herself go into Flossy Mae's body. She was living the very minutes that Flossy Mae had endured.

Suddenly bullets started showering down upon Flossy Mae and her children. The fear overtook every fiber of their beings. Flossy Mae knew the group was not chasing a run away because they did not have dogs with them. She did not understand what may have brought their vengeances upon her poor family. They had done nothing wrong. She had a permission slip from the Colonel to allow her and her family to visit her sister on another plantation. She knew this was a

84

most unusual permission and probably never allowed by any other slave master. She knew this would be unbelievable to the slave patrolmen so she was not so sure her permission slip would have worked with them anyway had they asked to see it. The problem was that they had not ask to see a permission slip. They had just started firing upon the sight of her family. That fact disturbed her badly. Why had this group not ask first as to why she and her children were walking along this road at night? Why had not one of these gentlemen parked his horse in front of her and said?

"Give me your permission slip!"
She did not understand. Then she remembered someone telling her that there were several poorer people who had now joined the ranks of the Slave Patrol. Some of these people liked the feeling of being as important as the large land owners or masters of the plantations. Many hunted just for the sport and Flossy Mae knew she and her five children were not of the right color to be given any kindness on this night.

As the group came ever closer to Flossy Mae and her family, her sixteen year old son said in a silent voice,

"Mother! That is not the Patrol! That is the Catchers!"
A relief came over Flossy Mae when she realized someone must have decided to escape. Her heart went out to that person, but she felt the group could not be looking for her and her family any longer. However, she knew she and her family were far from out of danger in any manner. Common knowledge was that a piece of property that she was considered to be, would be worth at least $1,500.00 on the open market. Maybe even more if the knowledge was given that she was a

house servant. Her oldest son may be worth even more than that because of his strength. Even the smaller children could bring large amounts at any auction.

Many rogues traveled with the catchers and the patrol of late. Those who wanted to make a quick penny would ignore the fact that the slaves would belong to another. They would often travel with their catch to even another state. An owner would have to know to where the slaves were taken to prove ownership. Some slaves had been branded with the plantations mark. Flossy Mae and her family had not. In many cases the slave owner would just believe his slaves had gotten away or that they were killed. Those killed in the proper manner would cause a reimbursement to be given to the slave owner by the government, but many had been sold or killed unbeknownst to their masters. All kinds of shenanigans had been happening lately.

Suddenly, a single shotgun shot rang out. Flossy Mae looked up to see a large man on a big brown horse standing high above her with his gun pointed straight down into her group. The man had hit her beautiful son. The man was so proud of himself. He acted as if he had just shot a prize trophy animal while her son lay in a large puddle of blood. Everyone could tell he was dead. Flossy Mae cried out. She screamed and she cried. She heard another man say,

"Shut her up!"

Having a good education and being quite intelligent, Flossy Mae knew she had to think of something really quick! She had to protect her other children. Her speech was impeccable. As the words started coming from within her, the catchers were taken aback. It sounded as though they were listening to a well breed blue blooded lady. She said,

"You have just killed a slave owned by the Colonel Winthrop Wayne. I have a permission slip for the group of us to be on this road. You are going to have to answer to the very powerful Colonel Winthrop Wayne, and I would not want to be in your shoes!"

From where, Flossy Mae could not imagine, did she get the nerve to talk to a white man like that, especially one holding a gun? It surely was from the grief of losing her precious son or the fear of losing another. She really did not know why she felt she could talk that way to anyone. One man took this very badly and he rode up to where she was now standing. He put the tip of his gun right up to her temple and he said,

"YOU SORRY WENCH! I should put a bullet through that tiny head of yours right now. Where did you learn to talk like that? Who taught you to act like a human?"

Flossy Mae felt her legs weaken. She had gone too far. She knew she had overstepped her boundaries completely! Suddenly, another man rode out of the darkness upon a buckskin stallion. He said in a very bass voice,

"Leave the wench alone. Let her be on her way. I know the Colonel."
He then barked,

"Rory, you are going to have a lot of explaining to do when we come in contact with that man. He controls most of this parish and I am very sure, as his wench has said, he will be most unpleased with this unfortunate accident."

"Accident!"

Flossy Mae thought.

"You murderers just killed my son."

Underneath her breath, she said,

"His son!"

Lyla awakened! What a nightmare. She was covered with sweat. Tears were flowing down both sides of her face and she was shaking uncontrollably. Dear God, she had just lived through a most horrible experience. She was there! She knew that she was there! That was her pervious life. How horrible was that? Dear God, she had just witnessed one of the most horrifying events that one human could do to another. Her body was shaking all over. She had lived that life! She was living it again with Flossy Mae. Her heart was breaking over the loss of her son! How could any human be so cruel to others?

After wiping away the sweat and the tears, Lyla tried to get some kind of control over her being. She lay awake for quite some time accessing the vision or the dream. Pieces of a puzzle were coming together. My God! She had just heard Flossy Mae say,

"His SON?"

Chapter 6

For weeks Lyla kept thinking about her last dream and that statement, "His SON?"

It hit her like a ton of bricks. Now she was starting to gain a new understanding. Flossy Mae had been a mother to some of the Colonel's children. Lyla had heard much about this. She had read somewhere that often the white women of those times would only have sex when they wanted to have a child. Birth control was nonexistent. Women were trained to not want to enjoy any sexual contact. This was a man's needs and wives were to be there when and if he demanded her services. But many of the conning women learned to use sickness or headaches to ward off any attentions their husband may give them.

Lyla had read about how often a master of a plantation would force himself upon his slaves. Actually, in reality he really did not have to force himself upon the women because the slave women were much aware of the fact that he owned them. He did own them! Therefore he knew he could do anything he wished to them. He could rape them. He could kill them or anything else he so desired. He could have sex right in front of a slave who may love that woman; yet with no recourse from that lover because he owned him too. The master could have sex with any or all of his slaves when and where he wanted. She was not aware of whether all masters did this, but she knew that this had been a common practice with many.

Lyla was so concerned with Flossy Mae to where she worried she may be taking over her life. She knew however, if she did not find out the truth and all the truth, she would never have any peace. The Flossy Mae period part of her person had come through to tell her something and she knew that she had better listen. Any person who would keep their years of life's experience in check so as to help their future self was worth listening to in Lyla's book Flossy Mae's experiences had traveled over a couple of hundred years to possibly save Lyla from having any such bad experiences. She knew she needed to know more. She had been through so much hurt in her life time. It now seemed minimal compared to the grief of the lovely Flossy Mae.

Flossy Mae's experiences compounded with her very own experiences were tragic enough. What happened in any of her other lives? Lyla knew if she pondered on that subject, she would surely go mad. Had they all been so very tragic? Had the Victorian self been murdered at a young age? From the knowledge that Lyla now had, it was starting to look like her being had always and always would have nothing but heartache and sadness. These thoughts saddened Lyla and she became very depressed.

In her life time, Lyla had seen so very many race troubles. She was but a child when all of the trammel was going on in the south. She had family in the Deep South. She remembered while on visits to see these family members, of how horrible it felt when she saw school children in a school yard screaming obstinacies to little black children as they walked down the street on the other side of a tall fence barricade. She remembers how horrible her family believed the white or black water fountains and the white or black bathrooms were. She can remember her father mistakenly taking her little brother up to a black water fountain, only to hear some big old Southern Bigot scream,

"Man what's wrong with you?"
She was alive when the lady refused to move out of her seat on that bus. She was alive when the college students, both white and black were killed. And she remembered that famous message by Dr. Martin Luther King from the Lincoln Memorial steps in Washington, DC. She also remembered seeing how horrible the poor man felt when the church was bombed in Birmingham, Alabama. She remembered noticing how he felt as if he may have caused the deaths of those beautiful little girls by his speaking out. Everyone could tell that he was almost destroyed when he had to give the Eulogy at the little girl's funerals.

Yet somewhere back in Lyla's time, all of this just seemed to be a black problem. Not until these later years had Lyla truly felt the pain. She was watching TV one day when she heard the powerful sermon that the famous Dr. Martin Luther King had given on that day when thousands upon thousands of people gathered in a peaceful gathering in the Capital City. This time, with her age and maturity she could feel cold chills running down her spine. The hair actually stood up on her arms when she felt the depth of that speech. Why had she not felt so moved before? Was it her youth or a practice of so much non-caring from those around her? No, it was more than likely because communications were not what they are today and Lyla could not remember hearing all that much about everything. She was aware it was going on, but she did not hear about it on a regular basis. Nothing was ever told to her in detail, until now.

Lyla always knew her family had not been prejudice in anyway, but she also knew they did not deal much on the subject. There was no hate there, but Lyla felt there may have been a few underlying feelings of white supremacy. Not intentionally of course, but something inside each person possibly came from all of those years of tyranny. She knew that she had descended from different slave owners and a mixture of other people of several nationalities. Although she had some interest in these things, youth got in the way of ever trying to find out many truths.

While working with her good friend Ina, Lyla's company had worked with President Clinton's office to hold a vigil and a play. The play was about a slave girl who had escaped to her freedom. This play was held in a Victorian theatre. This was during the year of 2000. Lyla and her co-workers had traveled to a small village to celebrate the years of freedom for the African Americans. There were only about two percent of African Americans in that community, but this is where it all had happened. This is where the southern slaves ran to freedom. They had crossed that river and traveled to Canada by the use of the Underground Railroad. The festival held was called,

"Two Thousand Lights of Freedom."

There were 2000 candles passed out and 2000 people lit those candles. Thousands sang and marched along the river banks in the very same spot that so many had managed to cross into freedom those many years ago. This was the community she had chosen to live in for a while because she had family living there when she ran from the despair of losing her beloved husband. Lyla's oldest brother was an artist and he lived in this community. He had painted a picture of the old church that had been built by a slave and showed slaves coming out of small boats up onto the banks of the Ohio River. He then directed their path to the safety of that church. His wife was a lovely gospel singer. She had started a song in the silence. She sang 'Amazing Grace,' and the whole crowd joined in. A singer was performing from a gazebo in the park but the sound system had not carried down to the banks of the river.

Lyla remembered the soothing sounds as the beautiful singing voices echoed up those river banks. There would have been no singing during the long ago escapes. There could have only been silence in fear of being seen or heard. Lyla felt the beautiful singing honored those whose voices had been silenced so many years ago.

This festival was most engaging to Lyla. She had enjoyed helping with the event. Many people of all colors had joined together in the city park that faced that river while they celebrated freedom. This settled deep within Lyla's feelings at that time, just as another gathering had done just one year later for those who had fallen with the 911 bombings. A vigil was also held in this small town's park by the river for those lost in the towers, the plane victims and the victims at the U. S. Defense Department at the Pentagon. Both of these events of coming together would always hold warm spots in Lyla's heart. She was so fascinated and her faith was renewed in the human race with all of the love and the prayers that was said on both of these occasions. She could remember the amount of tightness that people on each side of her body had given when they held her hands. Everyone was showing so much affection over both of these causes. She was thankful to see this comradely at each occurrence. This was so unlike it would have been years ago for so many white and black people. Lyla's thoughts were that of how wonderful it was that time had changed everything. She was so very thankful that these events for the town's people had traveled through the years of healing with a most blessed union. She hoped that Flossy Mae somehow saw these events through her eyes.

After leaving the fulfilling position in the northern state, Lyla had ended up in what she liked to call a la-la land. She floated from one simple job to another. She moved and then she moved again. She had lived in many of the states in the Eastern United States. Thankfully she had finally figured it was time to go home after much persuasion by her children. That is when she moved back to Nevada. Just as she had always believed, this must have been meant to be. Otherwise she would have never met her handsome stranger. After many visits, Lyla learned that her new man was a rancher. He had a large ranch in the State of Mississippi. She had noticed he was very powerful and forceful in every issue, but she felt softness about him as well. The two were becoming very close over a period of about a year while having a long distance relationship. Lyla was finding herself thinking of the possibility of a life with this good looking man. She knew she was enjoying everything about him, but could not figure out how they could ever have a life together with the distance between their homes.

Lyla was not without her other worries about the handsome new stranger. He was slowly telling her of his past. He told her of the many women he had been with in his life. He said he did not want her to hear any of this from anyone else. She found that he had married and had children by two of these women; thus giving him the total of five children. She did not know much, but she knew that one ex-wife lived close to his ranch. He was in constant contact with this woman. He stated this was because of the children, but Lyla could not help but get a strange feeling when the couple would be out to dinner and he would receive a phone call from his ex-wife. She saw something that would make one believe he was still married to her. However, she could usually tell from the drift of the conversation that the woman was most usually after money during these calls. Lyla could not understand this need with his first wife because all of their children were grown and with families of their own. Then while overhearing a phone conversation, she guessed the need for money was something regarding a need for one of the grandchildren. She guessed that was most probably the jest of their conversations. William had furnished each child with many horses and the tack to go with them. Obviously he furnished about any need they may have.

At the beginning of Lyla's relationship with this man, she did not have many of her reoccurring dreams. She was starting to believe these dreams were only brought on when she was lonely. She had always had so few dreams when she was happily married to her loving husband. Now she was so preoccupied with the fascination of this absorbing man. The lure in this man's aura was so strong to where she felt she had to be with him at all times and knew that she rarely thought of anything else..

William T. Jenson was a beautiful, big man. He had shoulders about an axle handle wide as people in the south would say. He was six foot five and a tower of a man. He had big hands, a big head and large all over was all one could say. Lyla joked and said,

"He was large and in charge."
Everyone believed him to be extremely handsome. Lyla only had one complaint at this time about the gentleman. That complaint was that she could not tell anything about William's eyes. She figured this was of his own making, because one could not see his true feelings while looking at him or see if he even had any feelings. This was because his eyes could often show no emotion at all. Lyla always liked to see someone's soul when she looked at them. This man was a man of steel and obviously his heart and soul were as well. Lyla knew he had willed himself, at some point in his

life, to never show his emotions. This, Lyla did not like about the man. Actually it scared her.

After dating for a while, Lyla must have taught herself not to look into her friend's eyes. Oh, she liked the looks of his eyes. They were pretty blue and deep set. He had a nice, sharp looking face. This man was indeed, extremely handsome. To this date, Lyla had not seen any coldness from this man. She only saw fun and comfort. Her only problem seemed to be that she could not read his eyes.

As time passed in this relationship, many times while on dates William would hunt out animal sales. This is what he was accustomed to doing and this is what he liked. He would take Lyla along. Lyla was not fond of the smells and of the dirt. There were also many farm type people who did not seem to mind stomping through waste and mud. Lyla was very often improperly dressed for this atmosphere. Something about the auctions made her feel uncomfortable. One night as Lyla was walking alongside her new friend, he stopped to explain the dollar value of a certain animal. He pulled her close to his body so people could pass by in the narrow pathway between the holding pens. She looked up to a most handsome, strong man under his large rimmed cowboy hat. This man was holding her and she felt she never wanted him to let her go. She felt so very safe in his arms. William was so not aware of Lyla's feelings right now. He was so involved in his thoughts and his conversation. He kept talking about his passion subject. He seemed to know so very much about each and every animal. He would become so engrossed in his explanations to where he seemed oblivious of the moment. He kept talking about animals without realizing that Lyla was idealizing his every move. It had been so long since this woman had felt safe in anyone's arms. She now felt that comfort and the security she so much enjoyed.

Chapter 7

The good Mr. William T. Jenson never stayed in Lyla's home town for more than three days at a time. His reason for being there was that he was either purchasing or selling livestock. He traveled wherever the animal sales or auctions may be. Sometimes Lyla would not see him for a month or two. She had now questioned the man as to what he was doing at her office on the day she had met him. He laughed and ask,

"Do you believe in destiny?"

Lyla laughed and said,

"No! Not really!"

He said,

"Well, I do! On the day I met you, I had tried to deliver a load of cattle to one of your local ranchers. I never realized your countryside could get so wet and muddy. When I tried to go into the buyer's field to deliver the animals, I could not get my truck and trailer in the fields because of what looked to be four feet of sandy mud. You know! That black oily kind you'al seem to have on frequent days. Someone had told me the construction site you were working at would have trucks coming in at all times during the day while hauling gravel. The person who told me this said he was sure I could find out who delivered these loads. With that information, I would be able to get some delivered to the muddy field where I had to drop the cattle."

Lyla laughed and said,

"Okay, maybe I do believe in destiny or fate! You have convinced me *or* that was the

99

biggest lie I have ever been told. I cannot tell by looking into your eyes. Has anyone ever told you Mr. Jenson that you have no soul?"

She then leaned over while putting her face directly in front of William's face and said,

"You have no soul Mister! You have no soul at all! I cannot see your soul!"

The large man only stared at her. She noticed he could stare for like forever without ever blinking an eye. Finally he laughed a big hardy laugh. This was all in fun, yet it was somewhat unnerving for the searching Miss Lyla.

After this fun weekend, William had told Lyla he did not know when he would be returning to her part of the country, but this time he would like to invite her to come and visit him. They left each other with the thoughts that they would call each other and make plans for him to visit or for her to go to visit his ranch.

That very evening, Lyla was feeling wonderfully happy. The couple had always made plans to go somewhere when William came to her town. Lyla always looked to find the perfect romantic food, the perfect romantic wine, even the perfect romantic clothing for herself. William always stayed in a motel and the two would always meet there. William had never been to her home.

Tonight Lyla was driving the distance home from the motel. William would be leaving at about four o'clock in the morning. She would not be seeing him again before he left. Lyla was now very tired. This had been such a wonderful and fulfilling weekend. She had such great fun. She believed that she would sleep like a baby on this night. She was getting very sleepy on her long drive home. She pulled into her garage and locked the doors. She stumbled through the house, luckily without falling over anything. She had only turned on one table lamp. It had been hours now since she had a glass of wine and she could not understand why she was so very sleepy. She smiled. Then she thought of how this was just happiness. This was complete happiness. Then she said to herself,

"You deserve it girl, it has been a very long time!"
She took a quick shower and headed for her bed. She pulled down the covers and slid her tired body between them. This night she would not remember when her head hit the pillows.

Somewhere in the night, Lyla started dreaming. When she awakened she felt as though she had dreamed the whole night long. She had just lived what felt like the whole childhood of Flossy Mae! Yet, she looked at a clock and it was still the middle of the night. Strange as this may seem she could remember every facet of this vision type dream. The massive dream started during the time period when the slave girl was a child of ten years old.

Flossy Mae had been but a child when she and the later famous Colonel had played together on the large plantation. One thing that had stood out in this dream was when Flossy Mae had shown Lyla a very hot summer day of her childhood. The slave girl had chosen to share that day with Lyla through her dream. All of the master male adults were either in the fields or away in town. The misses where surely taking their afternoon teas. Flossy Mae and whom she knew as Little Mr.

Wayne were playing around a huge old magnolia tree. This old tree was the largest tree in the front yard of this very massive mansion. The trunk of the tree was many feet around. On this day no other children seemed to be playing except Flossy Mae and Little Mr. Wayne. They ran around the tree for a while chasing each other, only to become exhausted in the heat. They both landed directly behind the tree on the side facing away from the house. The children were coming into a strange age. Flossy Mae was turning eleven that summer and Little Mr. Wayne was close to the end of his thirteenth year.

Little Mr. Wayne lay flat upon his back. Flossy Mae will never know why she did what she did but she landed her body right smack dab on top of Little Mr. Wayne. This was all in fun and usually nothing would have been thought about it at all, but at this time the youngster's youthful hormones were working overtime. Little Mr. Wayne put his arms around Flossy Mae in a vice type grip. He planted a great big kiss upon her lips. She remembered that she liked that and she kissed him back. They lay in that position for a while.

Then Mr. Wayne took off Flossy Mae's bloomers. She let him. Then he took off his pants. He laid his male body parts up against Flossy Mae's female body parts and both children seemed to like this comforting zone. Nothing else happened. The two just laid there with their bare bodies touching. After a few minutes Flossy Mae jumped up and put her bloomers back on. Before

Little Mr. Wayne could get his britches back on, Flossy Mae had taken off towards the closest barn. She screamed at him, while laughing and looking back over her shoulder,

"Catch me if you can!"

During these innocent years of childhood, the differences in the stations of life did not seem to be so prevalent. Oh, Flossy Mae knew that she was born a slave. She knew she lived in the little house and Little Mr. Wayne lived in the great big house. She knew that Little Mr. Wayne's father was her master, but she did not know the shame and the hurt she would face as an adult.

To this date, life on this plantation had been pleasant for everyone who lived upon it. Little Mr. Wayne's father was strong with his words, but he was a big hearted gentleman. In his later years, after he was not able to tend to his crops and animals, he would often sit out under the trees in a large rocking chair. The kind old gentleman did not seem to mind all of the children frolicking all around him. Black or white, the old gentleman seemed to enjoy the child's play. He had always treated his slaves nicely. This was of course as long as they did what he ask. Most all of the slaves on this plantation respected the elder Wayne. They even liked him.

Life was hard work upon this plantation, but it was also wonderful. Flossy Mae's mother and others kept the place spick and span. One could eat off of the floors in the mansion or in the cabins. Everyone worked hard and everyone seemed to be fairly happy. Flossy Mae had a sister whom the master had named Sassy. The reason she was nicknamed Sassy was because she was *sassy!* Her true name was Gussie but after the nickname was used so much, she was known only as Sassy! She

103

would often sass the master when she was but a child. As a whole, the black families had been allowed to stay together upon this plantation, but the master realized after Sassy had become a teenager that she was too much for his kind manner to handle. He had sold the wench to a neighboring land owner. Both masters had allowed the families to visit this sister upon occasions.

As the master's children and the slave children were becoming of age, things changed between them. The master's children were being trained to be masters and the slave children were being trained to obey. Flossy Mae and Little Mr. Wayne hardly spoke after that day around the old magnolia tree. Possibly, Little Mr. Wayne was embarrassed over what had happened, or he was just coming into his own as an owner of this great plantation. He had since been sent off to train as an officer of war and was gone from the plantation for several years. Upon his return he was known as Colonel Wayne. He also had a wedding in the planning stages. He was to marry the lovely Miss Rosalie Phelps from two plantations down.

Flossy Mae, being of age at this time was working as a house servant the same as her mother. The Colonel barely spoke. He had realized his station in life at this point and all feelings of childhood were gone.

A beautiful wedding was held. Flossy Mae did not attend of course. The wedding was held at the pretty young lady's home. The bride was only introduced to the help upon her arrival at the

Wayne plantation. The slaves were to help her while she prepared for living in her new home. The new Mrs. Wayne was to be the master lady of the house in some distant future. The day the elder Mrs. Wayne would pass, the younger Mrs. Wayne would be in complete charge. Each slave knew that he or she must learn to follow each and every rule that Miss Rosalie would put before them.

Coming from a stricter plantation, Miss Rosalie could be sharper with her orders than the members of the Wayne family. She could often be downright hateful. Flossy Mae had lived long enough at this time to know that many of these plantation owner's children were spoiled beyond all hopes of ever growing up. Gee whiz, they did not even have to dress themselves. That was done for them by a slave. All they had to learn was to shout out orders. To this date, Flossy Mae had never resented any orders given to her by the Wayne family, but she was finding her feelings to be more that of her sister Sassy's towards the Miss Rosalie. At first she did not like the new Mrs. Wayne very much at all.

After some time, while being reminded by her wonderful mother, Flossy Mae realized she could get more kindness from someone with honey than she could with vinegar. She began showing complete kindness to the new Mrs. Wayne and it worked. The two young ladies, being that of about the same age, became some sort of friends with the limitations of the stations one had in life. Flossy Mae obeyed every order given her and Miss Rosalie started being kinder to her. This was the way their relationship went.

One day while searching for a dress for Miss Rosalie to wear to a ball, Flossy Mae saw a light beige lace dress that she adored. She knew she could never have anything like that upon her back, but she could not help but stare at it. To her complete surprise, Miss Rosalie asked her if she liked that dress. She said,

"Yes, I surely do Miss Rosalie!"

Miss Rosalie remarked,

"I haven't worn that old dress in years and I really don't care much for it. I will tell you what. If you will hide it deep within your bed, I will give it to you. You will only be able to try it on when no one else is around. If you should ever be caught with it, you know the masters will believe you have stolen it. So, be very careful!"

Flossy Mae did not understand and was completely worried that she may be caught with the beautiful gown. However, something inside of her could not help but accept.

Miss Rosalie told her to put it on in front of the large mirror in the bedroom. This must have been a playful day for Miss Rosalie because she was being so very nice to Flossy Mae. This in itself was a worrisome deal. What if this master lady did not care for her and was only trying to set her up for a beating? The desire to put on the beautiful dress overcame any fears that the young slave girl had. She quickly put on the dress and stood before that mirror while admiring the beauty of it all. She left the dress on for only a few seconds. Suddenly, she felt complete fear overtake her being. She immediately removed the dress from her body and quickly put her uniform dress back on. Then she started to walk out of the room without taking the dress. Miss Rosalie said,

"Aren't you forgetting something?"
Flossy Mae said,

"I thank you Miss Rosalie for letting me try on your dress. I know I could have never in my life time been able to feel that wonderful material upon my body. For that, I thank you. Thank you so very much!"
Then she said,

"I can't take your dress Miss Rosalie! I could only get in trouble and I could never put it upon my back again."
With that statement, she ran out of the room. Miss Rosalie hollered after her in a nasty tone of voice,

"Come back here Flossy Mae!"
She turned and went back into the bedroom. Now, a mad Miss Rosalie said,

"What do you think you are doing by refusing my gift? You _are_ going to take that dress!"
By now she was screaming hatefully. She screamed,

"Do you honestly think I would put that nasty dress back upon my body after a black wench like you had it on?"

Flossy Mae could feel hot tears form in the corners of her eyes. She knew she must not let the master lady see her cry. This would be a sure sign of giving the master lady permission to be nasty with her at all times. She felt this happening was only a saddest condition of many of the whites.

Knowing that she must do as she was told, Flossy Mae reached down and gathered up the crumbled dress from the floor. She folded it neatly and carried it over her arm out of the bedroom door. As she closed the door behind her, she wondered what to do next.

As Flossy Mae left the mansion with the dress in tote, she did not know what to do. There was a large fire burning just past the largest cotton barn. This was a fire that Colonel Wayne had ask his slaves to start to burn a large dead tree that had fallen during the last big rain storm. She looked all around to see if anyone was watching her and she took the beautiful dress out to the fire. She rolled it up into a small roll and slid it way back under the limbs of that tree. She put it in the hottest part of the fire while she felt the heat upon her face. Still feeling it may not burn completely before someone saw it, she took a large stick and pushed it even further back into the coals of the fire. As she watched that beautiful dress burn, she stood there and cried. Large tears dripped off of her face as they fell down over her large breast. She could almost hear them hit the stiff, white starched material of the dress. She could not remember ever before crying this hard.

Oh, the degrading of it all. That was surely all Miss Rosalie was trying to do. She was surely trying to show Flossy Mae how unimportant her life was to anyone. No one in the Wayne household had ever been that cruel. Oh, everyone knew their places, what their duties were and so on. But everyone, masters and slaves alike were most usually fairly nice to each other. This was all new territory to the young Flossy Mae.

Lyla woke abruptly when her little dog barked at a noise he had heard outside. She was once more shaken with this ever so real dream. She checked to see what her dog was barking at and when she could find nothing, she went back to bed. To her amazement she could not go back to sleep. She knew she could contribute this to the very long dream she had this night. She was now so very wide awake, but she was still very tired. These dreams did that to her. She stayed awake for the rest of the night. She called William a couple of times, who wondered why she would be awake at these hours. She was comforted in the fact that he was driving somewhere and would be awake for the whole night.

Chapter 8

Weeks passed for the lovely Lyla. She was happy with her humdrum job and happy to be near so many of her family members. She enjoyed every minute of their company. She attended church on Sunday's with her mother and usually took the aging widow out to Sunday afternoon lunches at the few choice restaurants of her mother's town, Lyla's hometown. All was fine with the also widowed Lyla. She would allow herself to cry often. She still grieved over the loss of her wonderful husband, but by now she was ready to go on. As one in the south may say,

"Take that bull by the horns and just keep on going!"

Lyla had always been a strong woman. At least that was the face she wore for the whole world to see. She was so thankful for her friend Ina and her help with getting her the meeting with her sister. She knew that she would surely be insane by now had she not gone to Alaska. She also knew that now she was a firm believer in reincarnation! There were no doubts in her mind anymore. Her other entity, Flossy Mae had made a firm believer out of her. No one could create those scenes in a dream. No one could have the reoccurring dreams that Flossy Mae was giving her. She felt that she was living Flossy Mae's entire life while in her dreams. She knew she was at least living the most memorable times of Flossy Mae's life. She did often call her dreams visions, because many times she was not sure she was even asleep. This was way too real. If she had lost her mind, she would have lost Lyla all together. She was very much aware of who she was in this life.

She also knew she could never, in a million years, tell anyone about this adventure. Not William, not her mother, not anybody. No one would ever understand.

She would often wonder what would happen if every life that she had lived over thousands of years should come into her dreams. If that would happen, then she would surely go mad. She was fortunate in the fact that she only had Flossy Mae. Flossy Mae was on a journey to correct some kind of a wrong. Lyla knew she must figure out what that may be in her lifetime. She was not going to let her soul be bruised again. The slave lady was in a protective mood and was going to do everything in her power to protect Lyla. Lyla knew this to be a fact, and she was very thankful that she could see Flossy Mae's life through her modern day eyes. How blessed was she? Just like the Shaman had said,

"So many people would love to have the gift that you have!"
Lyla was beginning to see the meaning to that statement. Yes, she did truly feel blessed with this wonderful gift that was given her. Religion would condemn her for her now beliefs, however she could not help but believe that she had been blessed.

One Thursday morning, William called Lyla at her work. He was at his home and he told her of how the weather was beautiful and he wished she were there. He invited her once more to come to his ranch for a stay, as he would say. This time she agreed to come. She added that this was with a few stipulations. One stipulation was that she would have to find out first if she could get off work. She also needed to buy plane tickets since she had no desire, nor the time off from work

112

to drive the long distance. William listened quietly. Lyla knew him well enough now to know that he was getting a charge out of her demise. She could see him sitting there with a twinkle in his eyes and a rotten childlike smile upon his face.

Once back to work, Lyla's boss was very kind. He usually let Lyla do about anything she wished. She was extremely over qualified for her position. Her boss knew this and he would do everything in his power to keep someone with her knowledge. He told her to go, as long as she would hire a temp while she was gone. He added that he wished her to teach that temp what she needed to know before she left. He laughed and then said,

"Go have fun with your big cowboy. Stay as long as you wish! Your job will still be here when you get back."

When she stepped out of his office and was just about to shut the door behind her, she heard him say,

"Isn't love GRAND!"

Lyla stuck her head back around the corner and said,

"What did I just hear you say? Who said anything about love?"

They both laughed and the boss said,

"Lyla, I just hope you know what you are doing. You can stay as long as you wish, but don't make any sudden moves! Give that relationship some time to simmer ole' girl!"

Lyla answered with,

"Don't worry ye ole' head about it. I use my head for more than a hat rack every once in a while!"

As she was closing the door, she smiled at her boss and said,

"But thank you for worrying about me!"
She did appreciate his concern. She knew that she and her boss had become rather close friends over the time she had worked for him and she enjoyed that friendship.

Travel plans were made and Lyla took off for the southern part of the United States. In the great State of Mississippi, she had never spent any time. She knew absolutely nothing about it. She was thankful that William's hometown had a Marriott in it, even though she had been invited to stay at the ranch; she had thought the better of that. None the less, William met her at the airport. He was so happy to see her. He told her that he did not like the long distance between them. Lyla left that statement hanging in the air because she knew there would never be a way she could live in Mississippi. She also knew that this settled gentleman could never move west. He had stated that he was born and reared right on the very same spot that he now lived. She knew from the start that they were headed for a disaster with this distance between them.

What had started out as only fun dates had become something more serious by now? Now, is when the complications were to begin? Lyla was just going to be sure that she did not let herself get totally involved. She told herself she was dating because she could! She also told herself that she was dating to be sure that she would not die of loneliness. So she was trying to tell herself that this was only therapy. She often had long talks with herself. She would tell herself that she was dating just for the fun of it. She would tell herself that she did not have a problem being alone. She surely could not complicate her life with a strong, controlling southern gentleman such as the Mr.

William T. Jenson. Number one, he lived entirely too far away from Nevada. Number two, she was happy to be home and she was enjoying being with her family. Number three, William's personality was so very strong that he could overpower the weaker Lyla in every way.

Lyla felt that if she was around William for any length of time she would surely lose her identity completely. That was just the type of a power this man had in his aura. This would be most uncomfortable for a lady of dissension. No, she told herself, she was only having fun with this *VERY* handsome and very *SEXY* man. She was an adult for God's sake, and she had desires. She wanted certain things and this big strong man could certainly deliver certain things!

It was fun to travel to be with William. It was also very nice that no one in her hometown knew this gentleman. He was a stranger to all, and Lyla liked it that way. She had made plans for this to be a wonderful week and she was going to make that happen. Upon arrival, she did notice that William seemed to be overly happy to see her. She knew she could not usually read him in anyway but she was pleased that she could tell that he was happy that she was there. He told her that his cook had prepared a nice meal for the couple. Lyla was surprised at that statement as she thought,

"He has a cook!"

He had never mentioned this before. Actually, he had never mentioned much about his home. Lyla was impressed. Little did she know that she was in for many, many more surprises? When William walked her to his so called car, she saw that they would be riding in about a $200,000 (Two hundred thousand dollar) truck. The big man threw her suit

115

case into the luxury back seat that was covered in the finest of leather. Lyla looked at the tall steps and said,

"Sorry Bud, but you will have to lift me up there! I think I am a little short on one end!"
William laughed and hit a switch on the dash of the truck. When he did that, the running board of this large truck came down to where her feet were. She just stood there for a moment. William said,

"Get on!"
By get on she was not real sure of what he meant, but she stepped onto the running board that lay there before her. Once both feet were on this platform thing, William pushed that button again on the dash and the steps started to lift her up from the ground. These were elevator steps. She had never seen anything like that in her life. William, with his bigger than life size and his bigger than life good looks, was also driving this bigger than life large truck. He had to be a site that not many would ever be blessed enough to even see.

William was dressed in ranch clothing and Lyla was beginning to believe this is the only way that he ever dressed. Oh she could tell that each of his Wrangler shirts had to cost a fortune and that his neat, tight jeans were only of the very best of quality. He wore a ten gallon, very expensive western hat and the finest of cowboy boots. He was truly a site to behold.

One thing that Lyla loved about this man was that he was very comfortable in his own skin, or in his clothes as far as that goes. She had remembered many people in her neighborhood looking at him strangely when they would be out somewhere. He looked so different and so not from around there. William had acted as though he did not notice the stares. She figured he
116

thought as though the people staring at him were the weird ones.

Lyla remembered one night, when she and William had gone to one of the finest of restaurants in her home state, of how everyone was dressed in suits and ties. The ladies were in all of their finery. She had dressed in a nice little black evening dress. One which flattered her figure quite well and made her feel as though she had dressed appropriately for the occasion. She had worn the tallest of black high heels in silver and a silver color purse. She was a tall woman anyway and found great pleasure in being able to wear high heels with William and still have to look up at him. She was taking advantage of this fact and had now purchased many pairs of the really high heels she had always loved.

William had worn a suit jacket, but not one from Lyla's planet. His jacket was of fine suede and it had a braided designed yoke in the back of it while it covered those broad shoulders ever so tightly. The jacket had darker patches that looked as though they had been ironed on upon the elbows. Then he wore a pair of dress jeans and the very finest of alligator cowboy boots. Lyla realized as he sat down that he had a belt on that matched his boots, also made of alligator. Upon this belt was a large silver and gold western buckle, most likely made of silver and gold. His choice of a tie was a rope type thing that was held together with still another gold and silver medallion.

Lyla realized that William probably had on at least three thousand dollars' worth of clothing. Regardless, this was not the usual clothing of her small town. Gee, for her state as a matter of fact. In this man's large powerful presence, Lyla

117

laughed when she thought of how everyone who saw him probably now wished his style was their style. His larger than life presence just demanded that kind of respect! No one would dare to believe his attire was not the proper attire. Most women could not control their staring with admiration, while most men dropped their eyes as if they somehow felt inferior in the presence of this large powerful man.

William's way of dressing did not trouble Lyla. She thought he looked gorgeous! He was definitely a man who could pull this look off. Who could question this large man about anything? He looked the part of being in complete unadulterated control. She kept noticing that most of the looks given her handsome stranger were that of admiration. She just could not get over that. Most men only wished they could look like that and most women melted away when they saw this 'ALL MAN' walk by. Lyla felt so very proud to walk along beside of this very handsome man.

Lyla's mind went back to a time while in another hometown restaurant, sitting all alone, just awhile before meeting William. She remembered seeing a tall good looking couple dressed to the nines. They had breezed by her table in their fast long strides and they looked so confident and wonderful. Lyla had felt a jealousy when she looked at them. She felt she had been cheated. Then on nights with William she felt pride boil over inside of her while knowing that she and William were demanding that very same kind of presence. She held her head up high because she knew as a couple she and William were the kind of people everyone envied. These nights pride was playing a big part in the relationship. Lyla had felt a pang of quilt for being so proud! She just could not help it though, she was so very proud to be seen with Mr. William T. Jenson!

Now in Mississippi, the couple rode out of the city and onto a country road. Lyla could not help but notice that this was a nowhere land. William was very talkative and Lyla could tell that he was very happy that she was there. She could not help but notice the excitement in his voice when he was telling her of all of the things he wanted to show her. She looked out of the window to take in all of her surroundings. She could not see any houses, <u>anywhere</u>! They drove for what seemed like hours until finally William turned on his signal lights. He was turning right. Just before the turn, Lyla saw a very large arched gate to her right. Above the gate was a huge cast iron sign that said,

"<u>THE JENSON RANCH</u>!"

Lyla was impressed! She was very impressed! This man obviously lived a very nice life.

Lyla had once owned two beautiful homes herself. This was while her husband was still alive. She had not done without any of the fineries of life during that marriage. Her life had changed so very drastically with her husband's sudden death. Even with this, Lyla still had an air about her that showed the whole world that she thought that she was somebody. She had no money to speak of at this time. She often just barely got by, but she kept that air about her. She walked proud and held her head up high. She realized this was most surely the reason William had felt comfortable with her.

As the large truck creped slowly up the long tree lined driveway, Lyla could see the house in the distance. The site took her breath away. My God, she thought, he lives in a *SOUTHERN*

MANSION! Things kept going through her mind. She thought,

"You know he never brags! I knew he had nice things but WOW! This man never told me! Now who's out of place?"

Lyla suddenly felt inadequate. She surely must get over these feelings. If it showed, William would not wish to be around her. She must get a hold of herself and show her class. It showed very plainly that William did well for himself, but never had money been mentioned. William must be *very, very, very* rich! Oh God, he must be a descendant of a *very, very* rich plantation owner. William's home was a site to behold. Unlike the mansion she had seen in Louisiana, this home had been very well maintained. It was absolutely lovely. It looked like it had just walked out of a history book. Never had Lyla seen anything more beautiful. She was so relieved to believe that she and William were only playing at their relationship. Seeing this place only convinced her more of that fact! What would a man like this want with a humble girl like her?

Lyla would be most worried if this was anything more than for fun. After knowing about Flossy Mae, if it were more she would have to have a talk with this big strong man about his beliefs and his superior teachings. All that was wrong with the south had probably been instilled in this man's mind by his many generations of superiority! She was sure the touch of arrogance she had seen from time to time had been born very deep inside of this truly *SOUTHERN MAN!* The recent knowledge Lyla had gained with her finding out that she had been a poor black slave girl in a past life only intensified her worrisome feelings. Now she was sure that William and any of his past

120

lives most likely had always been a large land owner or even worse yet, 'A Master'! William said,

"Are you okay? I was hoping I could impress you just a little bit with my property. You seem worlds away!"

Lyla let out a little nervous laughter when she told William that she was just a bit tired from the flight, but that she really, truly loved his place. Then she sank back into her soft luxury seat and realized how silly she was being. This was a wonderful man who just happened to have a wonderful place. Obviously he **_was_** very rich! No matter, she was going to enjoy his company for as long as he was willing to give it to her. She also knew she must snap out of her total shock before she reached the house. As the two were stepping down from the large truck, William said,

"I wish you would let me cancel your hotel room. My house is very large with many quest rooms. I have house servants just the same as the hotel would have and my kitchen can be open at all hours. If there are times during your visit that you want complete privacy, you will never know that I am even here."

Lyla hesitated for a second. This was just long enough for William to take charge. He reached over his seat and picked up her luggage and said,

"Well okay then, I am certainly glad that is settled!"

Lyla stepped down from the truck and wondered as to what just happened there. She had not answered this large and in charge man, yet he had taken complete charge of the situation before she could think the matter over. She could only smile as she followed in the fast footsteps of her handsome host.

As William kicked the large double doors open upon the front of this beautiful home, Lyla was in awe! She stepped onto marbled flooring and looked up to see one of the most beautiful winding staircases she had ever seen. It was one of such a kind that she had only seen in movies. Large beautiful paintings and tapestries lined the walls and large pieces of antique furniture were placed tastefully throughout the foyer.

Just then a butler or a male servant, Lyla would not know the difference between the two, approached the large William. He said,

"Let me get those Mr. William. What room would you like the Missy to be in?"
William answered with,

"Put her in the left wing please. Put her in a room that opens out onto the upstairs terrace overlooking the gardens. I want her to enjoy her view."

As Lyla followed the butler to her room she heard William say,

"Rest awhile Lyla, I've got a few chores to do. We'll have dinner at 6:00pm. Someone will call for you. How do you like lobster? I took the liberty of telling the cook to prepare that for dinner! Sure hope you like it. If not I will have ready for you something else!"
She hollered back down the long stairs,

"Sounds wonderful William; I'll see you then!"

As the doors of Lyla's room opened, she realized that she had never in her life seen a prettier room. She thought,

"Well Dorothy, you're not in Kansas anymore!"
The suite was extremely large and painted in a sandalwood color. Large furniture was all about.
122

An antique, large open armoire caught her eye as the butler placed her suitcases in front of it. This large impressive piece of furniture was so beautiful and was covered with many carvings.

The other furniture in the suite was massive and beautiful as well. A chandelier hung from the center of the large high ceiling room. Plaster oval circles decorated the ceiling. In the middle of the large wall on the back of the room was the largest bed Lyla believed she had ever seen. It was high and it was large. A set of steps were provided to step upon it. Above the tall, massive head board were very long drapes falling from a large designed casing above. The bedspread was made of the same fabric as the drapes and it was so very pretty. She was not sure that she should even get up on that pretty bed. She hated to mess it up.

Lyla walked over to the large glass doors and walked out onto the terrace. Before her was a site that she knew she had never seen anything prettier in her whole lifetime. She had been to many places in the world. She loved England and had believed there could be no place prettier. She realized she had found that prettier place right now, because before her lay acres and acres of green. Just below the terrace were large amounts of beautiful flowers and statues. Everything seemed surreal and so peaceful in William's world. She could not help but wonder how William was so high strung, living as he did. He seemed so quick on the gun and somewhat stressed many times. Maybe there were duties and responsibilities around here that she had not had the chance to understand. But, looking at his beautiful home and his property, she could only see tranquility.

Lyla took many deep breaths and headed back into her room. She walked over and turned the knob upon her large double doors to lock them. It was only 3:00pm and there was a long wait until dinner, so she would set the alarm on her phone to awaken in two hours. She could use a much needed rest and this would help her to look good and be fresh for a wonderful evening with William. She walked over and lay across the bed and was asleep in a flash. Before she knew it, she landed head-on into one of her ever present dreams. Actually, it had been awhile since she had dreamed about Flossy Mae. Today even while she was asleep she realized this was not the time, nor the place for such a dream. She was agitated, even in her sleep, because the dream had shown itself on this wonderful week that she wanted to spend with William. A certain sense about her questioned as to why she would have a dream about Flossy Mae when she was on what she considered to be a happy venture or a holiday.

Chapter 9

As Lyla slept, she fell back into Flossy Mae's world. Breeding season had begun. Slaves were considered the very same as expensive livestock. Plantation owners were in the business to make money. They were also in the business of owning the very best of slaves. They wanted the strongest of men whom they called bucks and they wanted the finest of women whom they called wenches. The desire for their women slaves was that they could suckle their young for the lady of the house if need be. They wanted women who were strong and able to work long hours and carry heavy loads, yet be able to deliver strong and healthy slave children.

On the Wayne Plantation it was common knowledge that many of the slaves did get together in hidden places on every chance they could, but the breeding was a structured breeding process. The slave women lived separately from the male slaves. Big long houses were built for these reasons. Bunks were lining the walls of all living quarters. The women's quarters had large open fireplaces where they could cook. They cooked for their families and for the men. All children lived with the mothers until the boys became of an age. They would then be moved to the bucks living quarters.

A good slave birth season could bring a lot of money to a wealthy slave owner. If the slave owner cared for the growth of the slave until he or she was a grown teen; then if that slave had all of the qualities most owners would want, a slave owner could get up to $2,500(twenty-five hundred dollars) per slave. Many times a big strong buck could bring even more. These slaves were sold as livestock at open auctions. The Wayne Plantation sold many slaves each year, but they had several choice ones that they never sold. Luckily for the chosen slave families, they were never disrupted like so many others on other plantations. Those chosen ones and their children were kept for work upon the plantation for the most of their lives. Though not considered families and with no marriages and so on, this made it easier on some of the slaves. The groups were not disrupted for those fortunate enough to be in this very special stock of slaves.

In previous times, the specialty slaves were not bred with the deep field slaves. Many of those slaves did not even speak English. Many were purchased at the beginning of a planting season only to be sold at the end of harvest. Most of the house slaves and the specialty slaves had stayed at the Wayne plantation through generation after generation. Only rarely would a few be culled out and sold. As larger and larger families were birthed, the rules at the Wayne plantation were changing. Since the Colonel Wayne and Miss Rosalie had married, the line drawn between specialty slaves and field slaves had faded somewhat. Mum Charlotte was the only one left. The old master was long since gone. Flossy Mae knew that these changes were brought about mainly because of Rosalie's family traditions. In the last few years, all slaves were subject to breed and their off springs subject to be sold or traded.

Thankfully by now, Rosalie had come a long way with her treatment of Flossy Mae since that day that she had shamed her so badly over the lovely dress. She now seemed to be kinder to the slave girl. She had taken an interest in teaching Flossy Mae, while teaching her oldest daughter to read and write. Some of this was so the slave girl could help her with her studies, but Flossy Mae did not understand the other reasoning. She was only happy to know someone valued her enough to teach her such things. She also knew that Mrs. Rosalie could have been in great trouble if many people had known of this practice.

As breeding season was approaching, Flossy Mae let her mind go back to the days of her teens. She now knew the reason, but in those days she had not realized why she was not included in this event.

Lyla either woke up a little while questioning this subject, or maybe she had stayed in the dream that felt more like real time when she asked,

"Why? Why didn't they include you in the breeding? Was this because you were a specialty slave?"

Lyla could not get over the seemingly communication she could enjoy between she and Flossy Mae. It was as if Flossy Mae was answering her when she heard,

"No, once the elder Mr. Wayne gave his power over to the young Colonel, he did not follow the rules of his father. He either made rules of his own; or more plausible was the fact that he may have listened to his wife who had come from a stricter, much different slave and owner type relationship."

After that question, Lyla realized Flossy Mae would get to the complete answer somewhere in this dream. Flossy Mae continued by telling of how one week in the spring of Flossy Mae's 21st year, Miss Rosalie was making a traveling trip to another part of the state. It was planned for Flossy Mae to attend to the master lady to provide her with services. Colonel Wayne had insisted that Flossy Mae be the slave to attend his wife. Flossy Mae's mother was most usually the slave who would attend to such travels, but for some reason the Colonel had insisted that this trip was to be with the slave girl, Flossy Mae.

Flossy Mae could not help but wonder if she was not a perfect specimen of a slave girl. She knew that this week was the breeding week. She would once more be away. By the common standard of this plantation, a good specimen of a slave girl would be bred by the time she turned fourteen. She would deliver her first child at fifteen and one each year after. Flossy Mae knew the house slaves were bred more sparely, but she could not understand as to why she had never yet been included in the breeding. She had been of age now for six years. Each year something came up to where she was either to stay at the big house to care for a child, Miss Rosalie would become sick, the elder master lady would become sick or the master would just send her away for a few days. One year he had even sent her to the neighboring plantation to work with her sister in the cotton field for a week. She overheard someone say that the other plantation owner had been short on hands that week. She was more than happy to go on that venture because this caused her to have much fun talking with her sister for a whole week.

Flossy Mae seemed to have a need to feel wanted by some man by this age. Last summer, a buck named Samson had watched Flossy Mae every time she walked the distance from her quarters to the mansion. He had been the strength in front of a plow for many years until he fell one day while lifting the plow up onto a wagon. The plow had fallen upon his arm and crashed it. He had been such a valuable asset to the plantation owner to where the slave boss had brought a doctor to the quarters to fix Samson up. A doctor for a slave was most out of the ordinary. Therefore, Samson must have been a special slave to the Wayne family. The cures did not work and now the buck's arm was nothing more than a limp piece of meat from that day on. Colonel Wayne had changed Samson's daily job from heavy field work to the caring of the lawn. Samson was to keep all of the flowers weeded. He was to keep the leaves and debris off the lawns and rake and hoe wherever needed.

Flossy Mae would always speak to Samson. He would always speak back with a big white pearly smile. Shirts were not worn by the male slaves. They wore only a thin pair of white slacks that came just below their knees. They were then barefooted. Samson was black as coal and his skin shinned like glass in the sunlight. Flossy Mae found him to be attractive.

One late evening Samson waited while missing his dinner so he could talk with Flossy Mae. He stood behind the huge Magnolia tree that graced the front grounds of the mansion so as not to be seen. A thought passed through Flossy Mae's mind as to just how old could that Magnolia tree be anyway to be as large around as it was. Flossy Mae could see the big buck waiting for her. Even his big strong body was hidden from the house by the large trunk of the tree. She had a ways to go before she got to him but she knew exactly what he was doing. Being somewhat of a dreamer she wondered just how many stories that old tree could tell if only it could talk. When she started past the tree, she heard him say silently,

"Come here!"

She went over to him and he hugged her. He then planted a big kiss upon her face. Then he said in his broken English,

"I likes you girl! You're pretty!"

Flossy Mae was a little embarrassed, but she liked the attention. She had never been with a man and she believed herself to be long overdue. She liked the feel of his arms around her. Suddenly the meetings started to become a habit. The couple would grab a few stolen minutes wherever and whenever they could. They most usually met under that old Magnolia tree that had now become something very special to this couple. A romance had begun. Flossy Mae loved to be hugged and kissed by this big buck slave. They had never found a way to be together more intimately, but they both knew that it would be just a matter of time until they could figure out a way. Samson had started saying,

"You're my woman!"

Then one evening as Flossy Mae playfully skipped up to the large tree and threw her arms around her big buck, they both froze when they heard a loud voice scream,

"What do you think you are doing?"

130

It was the master. He was mad as hell and Samson ran just as hard as he could go to the bunk house. Flossy Mae, being less afraid of the Colonel Wayne, stood her ground. Oh she was afraid of this powerful man in the fact that he was her master, but she remembered the childhood days before they had become owner and slave. The Colonel had never been mean to her and she found it hard to worry too much about his actions. However, he seemed pretty mad at this moment!

The Colonel grabbed Flossy Mae by the arm, griping it until it hurt and he started walking very fast. He was a big man who was well over six-foot tall. His strides were so wide that Flossy Mae could hardly keep up without falling. He was very strong and had large muscles. Tonight he was being brutal. Flossy Mae was a petite little thing and she could not keep up with the large man and she fell once. The Colonel turned around the next time that she tripped. He reached out and he slapped her very hard across the face while he said,

"Keep up with me you trashy whore! You had better keep up with me if you know what is good for you!"

Flossy Mae could see fire shooting from the master's eyes! He was boiling! Now she was afraid! Her face was on fire from the slap and she was scared out of her wits. She had never seen her master in this way. Why was he so mad at her? Obviously it was her that he was madder at because Samson ran and he did not go after him. She tried to explain,

"Master, nothing happened. I swear nothing ever happened between Samson and me."

Once again the Colonel turned around and slapped Flossy Mae even harder in the face as he said,

"You mendacious, lying wench!"

By now her face was on fire on both sides and she was in total pain. The last slap was done with such force to where she was not sure he did not break her jaw. At this point, Flossy Mae did not know what to say or to do. There was really nothing she could do. Her owner was mad at her and who knows what he may do. He had every right in the world to kill her if he so desired. Was that what he was going to do? Flossy Mae became so-o-o very frightened as the Colonel dragged her to the large barn before them. By now he *was* actually dragging her completely, because he was moving too fast for her legs to catch up. She began to cry. The master just turned around and said,

"Dry it up Flossy Mae!"

He was talking to her as if she were a child.

When the master and the slave arrived at the now darkened barn, Flossy Mae knew there was no one else around. She knew she was in much danger. Suddenly the Colonel demanded that she climb the long ladder up to the loft. She could not see well enough to get straight on the ladder. She could feel the sharp blade of her master's long sword upon her hind side. Now Flossy Mae began to tremble. Colonel Wayne was going to hang her. That could be the only reason he was taking her up to the loft. She was quite convinced! He was going to put a rope around her neck and hang her from the top rafters until she was dead.

At this point, Flossy Mae cried more valiantly. She started begging her master to spare

132

her life. She begged and she begged with big salty tears running so hard down her face that she could not keep them from her mouth. She promised to **never** displease him again, and promised she would **never** speak to Samson again. The completely quiet Colonel finally spoke out when he said,

"You've certainly got that right Flossy Mae! You will **never** speak to Samson again. He will be sold at the very next auction."

With that remark, Flossy Mae felt saddened, but somewhat relieved. If the master should kill her then there would be no reason to sell Samson, unless of course he was just so very mad at the both of them that they both should be punished in the worst kind of ways.

Flossy Mae could not understand the master's anger. Many slaves upon that plantation had been caught while in the actual act of doing the nasty. None had been punished to this degree. Any that had become pregnant had been appreciated by the owners for delivering a nice healthy slave child. Could it be because she was a house servant? Were her standards supposed to be that far above the others? She just could not understand.

As the slave girl stumbled across some boards upon her arrival at the top of the loft, she could feel the Colonel behind her. She could feel the heat of his breath. She could smell his body. He was so very close to her. She could almost hear his heartbeat.

"Yes, Yes!"

Flossy Mae thought! He *is* going to kill me! Hot tears continued to flow over her cheeks. Just then her master reached around her with both hands. He got his fingers into the meeting place of her dress collar and ripped the front right off of her dress. She could hear the material rip under his strong grip. The master ripped her dress from the top to the very bottom, while ripping through the thick tight wide belt. The dress fell to the floor. Next she could feel a cold knife cut the ties to her bloomers. They too fell to the floor.

Suddenly the Colonel knocked Flossy Mae down to that floor. Thankfully there was a lot of hay or straw upon the floor of the loft that caused a softer landing, otherwise she believed her head would have surely busted in half. All of a sudden, Flossy Mae realized the Colonel was **not** going to kill her, just yet anyway. This realization hit her just as the large man bite down upon her lip. She could feel the hot blood run down her chin and onto her neck.

The Colonel took Flossy Mae's large breast into his hands and fondled them so very hard to where she could feel the pain shoot through her ribs. It was a very short time and then she felt what his full intentions were. A severe pain came inside of her as he penetrated deep inside and thrust his body between her legs. The poor girl had no idea what this was supposed to feel like. She had always heard it was nice, but all she knew at this minute was that she was in complete pain. Each time the large man would pound himself into her, she could feel her head banging upon that hard wood floor. Finally, it was as if a dam had busted when the Colonel finished. He must have been waiting for this sort of relief for a very long, long time, because he kept saying over and over,

134

"Yeah, Yes, Yes!"

Flossy Mae lay silently as tears flowed from each eye down into her hair. She had often thought of what it would be like to be with a man, but she had never expected anything like this. She had always cared about the Colonel and believed him to be a nice child who grew up to be a kind gentleman. Now she was wondering if the war training or maybe Rosalie had changed him so terribly much. Just as quickly as the Colonel had taken her, he dressed and told her to put her dress around her nakedness. He demanded that she head straight to the bunk house. As he started climbing down the ladder, he once more spoke in a very harsh voice.

"You, Flossy Mae are mine. *I - own - you*! You are my property. No other man, black or white is **EVER** to touch you!"

Then he said more softly,

"Do you understand me?"

Flossy Mae whimpered,

"Yes, Master, I do!"

Then she thought he had finally left but he spoke back up towards the loft again and said,

"Flossy Mae, this is between you and me! No one; and I mean no one is ever to know what went on in this barn this evening. Do you hear me? Now, do you understand that?"

Once more Flossy Mae said in a whimper,

"Yes, Sir, I understand!"

With that, the Colonel left the barn. It seemed like hours before Flossy Mae could even move. She stared at the moonlight coming in through the cracks of the barn. She cried, then she cursed and then she prayed. Thoughts ran through her mind as she wondered how that nice little boy whom she ran all over the plantation with could now be so cruel. Were white people and master's just forceful, hateful people? Then she came back to her reality and realized this is just the way it is. Even though as a child she had often wondered what it would be like to be white. She had faced reality in later years and once more she had to tell herself,

"I am the slave, he is my master. He can do anything he wishes with me. Just thank you Lord for sparing my life tonight!"

From that night on, the Colonel would make a time for Flossy Mae to meet him in the loft. She knew she had to go. She had no choice. Samson disappeared within the month, just as the Colonel had promised. The Colonel however, did not use the force he had used on that first night. Actually, he had fixed a small area for the usage at hand. He had placed a quilt upon the straw and made the place more comforting. He now had an oil lamp in the loft that he would light on occasion.

After about a month of constantly being used by her master, Flossy Mae adjusted. The Colonel was nicer to her now and would often talk to her some, either after or before the sexual act. He was often still very rough, but nothing like that first time. He had told her that he and his wife no longer had sex. Then in a more quiet moment he would tell of how he had wanted Flossy Mae way back when they were kids. He would tell of how he was sorry he did not take her then. There were a few times anymore when Flossy Mae could see that young friend she once knew. That sweet young child was buried somewhere very deep inside of this large forceful man. The Colonel had even apologized to a point over his treatment of her upon that first night. He excused his brutal actions by the fact that he was so very mad at the thought of Samson putting his hands upon her.

As time went by, Flossy Mae became happy to know she would be seeing the Colonel on their special nights. Even though she knew it was different than the love she had expected from a man. She knew she was either falling in love or that she had really always been in love with the man she knew as Little Mr. Wayne. Strange as this may seem, she got to the place to where she could hardly wait for the next visit. She looked so forward to the night he had ask for her to meet him. She was starting to get very strong feelings for her master. She always would know that he owned her. She would always know that no one on earth could ever know about them, but just the same she was starting to feel blessed and very happy. She started to believe that she was even loved by the powerful Colonel. Yet, she wondered how that could be. She was the slave, he was the master. But, many times when they were together she could see great tenderness in the big man's eyes.

There were times in the following year that even in the big house; the Colonel would sometimes give Flossy Mae a wink. Or he would catch her alone and pinch her on the butt or breast in a mischievous way. A couple of times he had brought her a trinket of some kind from the store. One day he brought some beautiful diamond earrings for Rosalie. Then he said,

"Rosalie, since Flossy Mae tends to you and is in the house to be seen at all times, don't you think we should dress her better?"

He had purchased a pretty pair of gold looped earrings for Flossy Mae. Rosalie agreed and handed the earrings to the slave girl.

Flossy Mae looked into a mirror that hung by the water cooler and saw the shining beauty. She bowed completely at the waist while she thanked the Colonel and Mrs. Wayne. Before very long Flossy Mae was ask to wear different uniforms. These uniform dresses were more stylish. Many had ruffles, some had bows or pleats. All were mostly white, but attractive just the same. Flossy Mae with her large breast, her tiny waist line and large hips, looked lovely in about anything the family put her in. Her only problem was that the other slaves were questioning her about her better treatment. Some were beginning to resent her. This too passed. Within a year, Flossy Mae was given a small room in the back of the big house. The Colonel had explained that his wife Rosalie had become somewhat ill and could not wait for Flossy Mae's help if she was way off in the valley at the bunk house.

Rosalie did take to her bed quite often these days. Some days she would not even come out of her room at all. The house was so very massive in size to where one could really get lost in it. At these times, the Colonel could sneak away into Flossy Mae's room and the two could have a constant relationship.

As time would pass, Flossy Mae became pregnant. She was scared when she realized that she was expecting. In her thoughts she was sure this would be the very end of everything. Her good life, her soft bed, her nice clothes and her happiness was all about ready to go up in smoke. To the contrary, all ended well. The Colonel seemed quite pleased with this event. He definitely was not *unhappy*. Rosalie was also satisfied that Flossy Mae had been bred by what she believed to be one of their special bucks. She knew this was common practice and accepted the pregnancy as she would any other.

On the day of the delivery, Flossy Mae's own mother helped to deliver the baby. She delivered a handsome baby boy. Flossy Mae was elated. She noticed when the Colonel looked upon the baby, he had a soft smile. She could not help but wonder just what this child would be to this man. Would he treat him differently, or would he become one of the field hands and a prized buck.

During one of the visits that the Colonel made into her room, Flossy Mae said,

"I'm going to name him Joshua!"

The Colonel smiled and said,

"That's good Flossy Mae. That is a good Biblical name and it fits him well."

While no one was looking, the Colonel reached down and gripped Flossy Mae's hand. She could see tenderness in his eyes. Flossy Mae turned her head over to the side of her pillow and sighed a sigh of relief. She realized that all was well at the Wayne plantation this day.

Chapter 10

Lyla awakened to the sharp sound upon her telephone. Had it been two hours? She had to look around a bit before she realized just where she was. With her strange dreams lately she was never quite sure as to where she may be when she first woke up. Gee Whiz, she thought, that was some dream. Flossy May surly came through very strongly today. Lyla was learning so much more about Flossy Mae's life and she was saddened for her. Looking at her surroundings, she realized that this was neither the time nor the place to worry about Flossy Mae, a woman who had been dead for much more than a hundred years by now. Why was it so important to this dead woman to tell Lyla her story? Why could she see it so plainly and why was she reliving that life?

Lyla questioned herself. She asked herself if in reality could she really be watching this historical figure's life? Once again she thought that maybe she was instead just losing her mind. Maybe this is the way it is when someone is losing their mind! She shook herself as she thought of how she only wanted to enjoy her time at this mansion in this day and time on this very special week. She wanted to enjoy the company of her own handsome boyfriend. She did not want to have to worry about a man who would be close to two-hundred years of age right now. She wanted any crazy dreams to just go away right now. Even if it was a true Flossy Mae, she wished her to disappear for at least a week.

Lyla wanted this to be a time for the living. She was in William's home and she was so looking forward to a wonderful visit. She must get dressed now and try to forget all of the problems of a past life. God knows she had enough problems of her own without going back hundreds of years to find more. She wanted to give her undivided attention to that wonderful handsome man whom she would see very shortly.

With that, Lyla jumped off of the very high comfortable bed and headed for the adjoining bathroom. Once inside, she was amazed once more with the floor to ceiling mirrors and the marbled floors. What beauty to behold! She whispered to herself,

"Now, I could get used to this!
Fun thoughts crossed her mind as she enjoyed every minute of climbing into the oversized bath tub.

Lyla soaked for what seemed closer to an hour instead of a half, while she gazed out of the small clear glass section of the beautiful round stained glass wall that was atop the back of the beautiful tub. There had been many bottles of oil and bubble bath upon the shelf that hung high over the tub. Lyla had chosen the Lavender smell soap, bubble bath and oil. She was becoming so relaxed to where she feared she may go back to sleep and let time fly away from her. Then she chuckled at the thoughts of how her host would feel if she just slept their dinner time away. What an impression that would make! Yet, she somehow knew that should that have happened, her charming host would have left her alone for her needed bed rest. Oh, how embarrassing that would have been.

No matter how soothing the bath seemed to be, Lyla knew she must get dressed. She had been to enough business dinners and enough social dinners of the elite to know that she must dress very formal on this evening. She chose a black dress that fell low in the back. Long sleeves were made of chiffon and the soft material of the body of the full length dress flowed down over her beautiful figure most elegantly. She then pinned her hair up into two buns on top of each other. She then fanned and pinned each bun out at the bottom. This style was simple to do, but so very elegant. Thankfully Lyla's smooth, pretty face could handle looking beautiful without any hair, so the tight pulling back of every hair only made her look sophisticated and sensational. She was so thankful a beautician friend had showed her this trick.

Lyla then reached into her bag and pulled out her beautiful diamond earrings. She had a necklace that boasted of a cluster of diamonds at the end of a chain. She hoped that she was going to look wonderful. She also knew that William had never seen her dressed quite in this way. She knew that she was dressing to impress. Impress this man is what she really wanted to do when she spent what she considered a high price to purchase this dress. Now after finding out how he really lived, she questioned as to what it may take to impress the apparently wealthy Mr. William T. Jenson.

Just as Lyla reached for her black satin clutch bag, doubts started to cloud her mind. Who was she fooling? How could she impress this man of distinction? He had definitely been around that block more than once. There was also the fact that he was very, very rich and she was very sure he had dated or been in the company of probably some of the most beautiful or best dressed women of the world. That old guarding her heart part of her mind came into play for a moment when she said to herself,

"We're only playing! He will tire of me soon enough! Besides how could anything ever work between us anyway with the miles we live apart?"

Why was she so scared suddenly? Was it the shock of the wealth William had? She surely knew after all of this time that the man was not poor by any standards. But, seeing this home, the ranch and that truck; Lord, who on earth drives a truck like that anyway? With his great wealth why was he not with one of those trophy girls that look like Barbie Dolls and those who would not care how old a man may be if he could keep her in the way she wished. Then she said to herself,

"Watch it girl! You've been called a Barbie Doll before yourself!"

Oh Well, she thought with her crazy sense of humor, at least he will know that I can clean up well. This comment cheered her up. Then she said out loud with an upbeat cheerful tone of voice,

"You had better like this dress! I spent a small fortune on it to impress you Mr. Jenson!"

One last glace into the mirror and Lyla opened the doors to the large hallway. She walked gracefully in her new high heeled silver glitter and black satin shoes across the beautiful Asian rugs. As she reached the top of the wide beautiful spiraling stairway, she could not help but think of the movie 'Gone With The Wind'. As these thoughts were crossing her mind, she took hold of the banister and started her long descent down the lovely stairs. She let a spring be in her heels as she let herself play act just like she was in a movie. She held up the right side of her long dress and floated down the steps while taking her time to glamorize each step that she took. She had been so into her fairytale performance to where she had not noticed that William was awaiting her at the very bottom. When she did notice him, she became red faced and she almost tripped. Thankfully, he did not seem to notice.

The handsome William Jenson was dressed in a wonderful black dinner jacket trimmed in grey. The black pants had a grey matching stripe going down each side. His beautiful graying hair was combed so perfectly. Every hair was in place. She had never seen him dress in this way. She tried to choke back the words, but too late, they were already out there.

"My God, you are handsome!"
She was not sure how this gentleman would accept such a compliment. Maybe he did not hear her in this massive area of the house. Now she was embarrassed.

As Lyla reached the third step up from the bottom, the tall Mr. Jenson reached out his right hand and took Lyla's hand into his as he helped her down the last three steps just like they do in the movies. Lyla wanted to pinch herself to see if she was really there. William then said, while speaking in almost a whisper,

"You look so very lovely tonight. You took my breath away as you walked down those steps. A more vision of beauty I don't think I have ever seen."
Then William pulled her close under his shoulder and whispered,

"You had better quit dressing like this lady. I may never let you go home!"

Then the suave nature of this man caused him to add in jest,

"Thank you for that compliment while on the stairs! I would like to ditto that to you Miss Lyla by saying; My God, you sure are beautiful!"

Well, thankfully the expensive dress did impress the great Mr. William and Lyla felt proud of herself for purchasing it. She could smell the sweet smell of William's cologne and she could feel her legs going weak. She knew that if she could not get over the impression that this man was making on her, then she just may never want to go home. Suddenly she got the nerve to say what she had wanted to say so badly to his face when she said,

"Let me say it so you can hear me, lip reader. You *DO* look so extremely handsome tonight Mr. Jenson! It embarrassed me when I did not mean to blurt that out a while ago like that!"

William laughed and said,

"I know!"

He seemed to find humor is just about everything. What a refreshing and charming man to be around.

All through dinner the servers came and went. Never had Lyla received such service in even the best of restaurants. The Jenson household cook or cooks provided the most wonderful of meals. The wine flowed, the candlelight flickered and the food melted in one's mouth. Lyla knew everything was delicious, but she could not keep her mind on the food, nor the wonderful expensive wine. She could only stare at the handsome

146

William T. Jenson. She noticed that he was having the very same problem of keeping his eyes off of her. She could still feel his touch from when he pulled her large dining room chair out from the table for her. She had noticed he lingered with his hands upon her shoulders. She could still feel them there. Lyla knew right then and there that there was no turning back. She was falling deeper and deeper for this handsome stranger. She could only pray that this stranger was not toying with her affections. She could only pray that he too had very deep feelings for her.

After a couple of hours of talking and enjoying the atmosphere of the beautiful dining room, William came over behind Lyla's chair and pulled it out. She got up and followed him to a seating room nearby. Thoughts crossed Lyla's mind concerning the fact that this wonderful man was such a total gentleman. It seemed the main words that kept crossing her mind this night was,

"I could really get used to this!"

William excused himself for what he said would be a minute and left Lyla gazing at the candle opera sitting upon the large medieval looking coffee table Then she jerked a little with her thoughts, when she thought of how she could not think clearly at any time that the handsome William was close by. It was as if she was swallowed up in his energy or something. Let him walk out of the room and it seemed her mind worked properly again. She questioned as to what kind of power this man had over her. It did feel as if she was under some sort of a magic trance the minute she came close to this handsome stranger. Then she laughed and thought,

"Maybe he is some kind of a warlock or something like that. Maybe he has put a hex on me!"

Lyla seemed to be in such a fun loving spirit tonight. Maybe it was her host. Maybe it was her lovely surroundings. Maybe it was because this beautiful mansion took her years and years back into the past. A past she had once believed to be gentler. As she looked at the large paintings and the beautiful old furniture, she wondered what kind of stories this old place could tell. Then she laughed again when she thought,

"No, No, No! If anyone was listening, I don't want to know. One continuing spirit is enough. Flossy Mae is more than I can handle right now. So please, if anyone is here don't come to me in any of my dreams. There is no room for you there. I have a full house. Besides, that would put me completely over the edge and I would be very sure that I was a certified crazy!"

A servant walked into the room and startled Lyla for a second. The sweet lady was only there to ask if she could get Lyla anything like a drink or something. Lyla said,

"No thank you!"
Then she snapped back into reality. She suddenly started having a serious talk with herself. She said,

"Lyla, you are moving way too fast. You both are moving too fast. This can never work. There is *NO* way this can work! You have a life many miles and many states away. This man is very stationary. He would never leave this place. Why would he? Who in their right mind would ever ask him to do that? He would be some kind of a nut job if he ever left this beautiful home and plantation!"

She had to laugh at herself when she realized that even in her thoughts she was mixing the old world with the new. She had just thought of William's ranch as a plantation. In these modern times people would laugh if they heard such things. She laughed to herself when she thought of how it would sound to say,

"Oh, I live on the Jenson Plantation just a few miles from town!"

She was getting silly. Maybe she had too much wine, but in reality Lyla knew no one should ever ask William to leave this beautiful place. So, she continued talking to herself by saying,

"This is not going to work Lyla! You came here thinking that you would just have fun. You are older. You know how to date. You know how to keep a wonderful casual friend or lover. You know better than this! Get this week over with then run, run, run! Run girl, as fast as you can. This man is so bad for your ideas of your perfect single life. This man!!!....you are falling in love with! He was only supposed to be a friend. With benefits maybe, but still just a friend! Get a hold of yourself Lyla!"

Lyla heard a voice say,

"Why the frown upon such a beautiful face? You shouldn't do that! You will cause wrinkles! Wrinkles should never be welcomed upon a lovely face such as yours!"

Lyla snapped out of it and turned to William and said,

"Oh, I was just thinking!"

William said,

"I know better than to ask any more questions when a woman says she is *thinking*! If you are through *thinking,* I thought maybe you would like to take a stroll with me through the gardens."

He reached around her and placed a shawl upon her shoulders while saying,

"The evenings can get pretty chilly around here at times."

Lyla stood up and said,

"That would be lovely. William you have treated me wonderful ever since I arrived. You have treated me like royalty and I thank you. I find I thoroughly enjoy your company and I have never visited a more beautiful home. I am going to be sorry when my visit is over."

William pulled Lyla close and said,

"That was the plan!"

The two laughed and William unlatched the large glass doors to the gardens. He then took Lyla by the hand and they strolled quietly out of the house. Lyla had never seen such beauty. Beauty was everywhere. She could not help but feel like she was in a dream or maybe in a movie. She was even questioning whether the large handsome man, William Jenson, was just a figment of her imagination. With her vivid dreams, maybe this was one of those as well. Maybe she was not really here! No man could be this perfect. No man could be this handsome. No man could have what this man has. No man could ever be that perfect of a catch if someone was looking. Yeah, that was it, she was dreaming. She had finally completely lost her mind. None of this was really happening. If she could conjure up one or two hundred year old people, well then she could certainly conjure up a man of her dreams. She thought almost out loud,

"Somebody pinch me!"

A cool breeze swept by and Lyla shivered. William reached over immediately and pulled her tall thin body close to his. She almost lost herself in his large arms. She felt so protected. She felt so comfortable in these arms. She felt that strong feeling of belonging. So, if this was a dream she was now praying that she never ever woke up.

The winding paths were all lined with beautiful flowers and shrubs. A statute would lurk out from the bushes ever so often. The shadows from the moon and the stars would make this world seem even more like a dream. Although this long walk had been a silent one, William finally said,

"Let's sit down on this bench over here for a spell. I don't know about you but I love looking at the stars. On my travels I am always happy to get back home and away from the cities so that the stars are visible."

Lyla scooted close to William when he reached out his arm to hold her. She could feel the beat of his heart. She knew this all had to be very real! She knew not why she could receive these blessings after all of the burdens of her life. Why had God given her the privilege of meeting this man? He came from worlds away. He was someone that fairytales were most surely written about. He was just too good to be true. This man was everything that any woman could ever want. He was everything any woman could ever dream about. He was the complete package. He was bordering dangerous on Lyla's stay away distant radar.

The couple sat upon that bench for a while. During this time William was telling Lyla the names of the stars. Both were showing each other what they knew about the skies. They joked and laughed when a small plane passed low above the trees. Lyla had said that maybe it was a UFO. This couple was having a wonderful time together this evening.

Before the journey was to begin back up the paths to the house, William took Lyla into his arms and their lips met. While Lyla was melting under the pressure of William's lips, she knew it was too late for her. She knew she could never turn back now. She was in Heaven. She was feeling things she had not felt in years. She was falling head over heels in love with this great big beautiful stranger. She would worry about the distances and the problems this relationship could cause tomorrow. Right now she was right where she wanted to be. Right now, she prayed this evening would never end.

Chapter 11

Lyla stayed in the State of Mississippi for five days and four nights. She had planned only three days and two nights but William had other things in mind. Therefore, plane tickets were exchanged and Lyla enjoyed more days upon that beautiful plantation. One evening William had taken Lyla to an outside country theater where the actors were good, the food was passable and the seating was uncomfortable. William had asked Lyla to wear jeans for this event, but she realized she had not packed any for her trip. So, that afternoon she got to see the downtown area of the closest town.

This quaint little town had stores that looked like they had just walked off of a Western movie set. This was so fitting because William seemed to always look like he had just walked straight off of a movie set. He always seemed to dress to fit exactly the way one would expect a person to dress to match their surroundings. Today, while walking down the wood planked sidewalks, Lyla smiled as she looked over to see her handsome William dressed in tight western jeans. He had on a western style, denim snapped down shirt, cowboy boots and a ten gallon cowboy hat. She laughed when she realized he was able to fit in anywhere he may go. She, on the other hand most surely looked completely out of place with her black pen striped pants, high heels and a silk blouse. She could not help but notice everyone was staring at her.

William walked with determination and with a hard, strong long stride. Even his walk told everyone that he was in charge. He looked and acted all the parts of being so very powerful as he breezed into a store and picked up Western wear for Lyla. William had said to the clerk, so matter of factually,

"Fix this fancy lady up with some hometown clothes, if you don't mind."

With that he had started walking out of the door. He looked at Lyla and said,

"I'll be back in a little while!"

And out the door he went.

The lady who was to wait on Lyla had a big smile upon her face. She was not a young woman but she wasn't all that old either. She had many pounds that she may not have needed, but her sweet round little face was all aglow with anticipation. She smiled at Lyla and said,

"Come on honey, let's fix you up!"

Lyla was asked her sizes and the lady pulled her half glasses up from a chain around her neck while she wrote down every word that Lyla said. Lyla just stood there in the middle of that store while feeling so very out of place. She felt that everyone she had met since being in this community looked at her as if they thought that she might break in half if they came any closer to her. She also could not help but wonder about other thoughts they may have. She was questioning as to just how many women that the Lord William T. Jenson had brought to his home for a love making week or weekend.

Lyla laughed under her breath when she thought of how in her mind's eye she was now calling the tall good looking stranger, Lord William T. Jenson. She somehow could not feel that a title such as Mister fit this large and in charge being. In her mind he should have been a Sir, King, Colonel or something besides just a Mister. She felt like a teen again as she thought,

"He's Lord William T. Jenson to me! I will call him Lord William!"

With those thoughts she laughed out loud. The sweet little lady clerk came running. She said,

"Are you okay Sweetie?"

Lyla laughed again and said,

"I'm fine. I am perfectly fine! Everyone around here is either wonderfully nice or I look like I am helpless. Which is it?"

The sweet little lady looked puzzled or bewildered but replied,

"Honey, I did not mean to hurt your feelings. We just are not used to seeing anyone around here quite as pretty or as frail as you. You are beautiful and so sophisticated. Of course we knew you would be. William would have had to have good taste. He is so pretty himself, don't you think?"

With that Lyla laughed. She then felt comfortable with the sweet lady and asked,

"Does Mr. Jenson bring lots of ladies into your store?"

The lady quickly answered with,

"**Oh my no** honey, never, never, ever! As a matter of fact I have not seen him with another woman since Sofia passed."

Lyla became shocked. She realized she did not know William all that well in reality and was very surprised that he too had lost someone to death. Obviously this detail was too painful for him to mention. She suddenly realized that neither one of them had gone into any detail about their past. Possibly both believed this was a passing casual

155

fun time to be with someone. But why would William invite her to his home community if he had not done this kind of thing before? Just as that thought waved across Lyla's mind, the lady said,

"Oh, we all know you are very important to William. Otherwise he would have never brought you home to meet everyone. Oh, we always knew he probably had dates with women in his many travels, but he sure had no intentions on letting any of his neighbors and friends know anything about that!"

With that statement the lady handed Lyla a big arm full of clothes. In the other hand she had a pair of cowboy boots and a white Western hat. Lyla smiled as she wondered just what she might look like in this getup. None-the-less she traveled the long length of the store to a dressing room and proceeded to put the clothes upon her back. Everything fit perfectly and staring back at herself in that mirror was a true cowgirl looking person. She put her hands down to her sides as if she was pulling guns out of holsters and said,

"Howdy cowgirl!"

While still laughing, she stuck her head out of the curtains and hollered at the clerk to tell her that everything fit just fine. Then she heard a deep sexy voice say,

"Come on out here and let us see."

As she walked a little shy out of the closet type dressing room, she pivoted with a complete turn right around and went back in. William spoke through the curtains and said,

"Get the tags off those clothes and leave them on please. We're going somewhere where you'll need them."

As Lyla stepped back out of the dressing booth she heard a loud whistle! William had a smile pasted all over his face from ear to ear. Everyone could tell that he liked what he saw. Like a little school girl, Lyla ran back into the booth to retrieve her things. She noticed that William had his arms full of still another group of the same kind of attire. He looked at her and said,

"Do you like these?"
She looked at him strangely, so he said,

"I want to take you riding tomorrow, so you will need two outfits."
He looked at her with a mischievous grin and said,

"Unless, of course, you want to go dirty!"
She laughed but said,

"Why another pair of boots and another hat? I would probably never have anywhere else to wear these things!"
William just glared down at her and said,

"Oh yes you will! Besides, I just think you look pretty in them!"
Lyla just shook her head in disbelief and pulled out her wallet to pay the clerk. The clerk looked at her surprisingly while looking up at the large Mr. Jenson and then said,

"It's been taken care of dear! Nice to have met you! Hope to see you again soon!"
With those words following the couple, William rushed Lyla out of the store as he hollered back,

"Thank you Miss Patty. You're wonderful, as always. Have a nice evening!"
Just as the couple stepped down from the wide wooden planks used for the sidewalks, Lyla noticed that William had moved the truck

157

somewhere. It was nowhere to be seen. She looked down the next block and she could see a large wagon being pulled by two large horses. Wow, what a site. Now Lyla knew she must be dreaming. She was back in history by years now. Or, maybe she was in the middle of a western movie. Gee this was fun!

The couple waited, as did other couples, along the walks for this horse drawn wagon to arrive. It made many stops along the way. When it stopped for them; William's helping her aboard was by just lifting her whole body up unto the large wagon. Suddenly they were bumping along a side country road while on their way to an outside theater. Lyla was very excited to be attending the unknown.

When they arrived at their destination, Lyla found that the only seating was to be bales of hay or straw. Each was covered with a colorful wool horse blanket. William led Lyla to some bales close to the front row. People were coming from everywhere. Other large wagons and horses were arriving. Lyla had no idea this event could be so large. She could see hundreds of people. Many were coming up and speaking to William. One old man came up and said,

"William, introduce me to your pretty new wife!"

It was funny as to how William did not correct that; but instead he just told the man that her name was Lyla. Everyone she met seemed to be most friendly and happy to meet her. William was obviously very popular around these parts. Everyone seemed to love him.

Lyla was excited with all the happiness and friendliness around her when William said,

"I'll go get us some popcorn and cokes because the show is about to start."

Lyla said okay and laughed as she threw her purse down on the other side of their hay bale. She then said,

"I'll hold your seat!"

This was so amazing. Lyla could not remember having this much fun. It had been years, and even then she had never done anything like this. William's world was so different. William's world was fascinating and seemingly much fun.

William came back while speaking to everyone along his way. When he sat down he handed Lyla her coke. Then he sat his drink down on the ground in front of him along with the popcorn. He reached into a saddle bag of sorts that he had brought along and pulled out a nice soft throw. He threw it over their shoulders and said,

"It's going to get cool in a bit!"

The show began with beautiful singing. Then there were three actors who had puppets and they could throw their voices into them. They were also comedians and everyone laughed for at least an hour. Lyla loved to hear the strong laugher coming from deep inside of her partner. Every so often he too was watching her and he would lean over and say,

"Lady, you have a beautiful smile!"

After the comedians, there was a play. It was also a comedy and great fun was had by everyone!

After the show, there were more introductions. Lyla hoped she would never have to remember any of the names of the people she had met. There were just way too many. She could look into William's proud eyes when someone would say she was pretty or she could feel an extra tight squeeze around her waist. She thought of how these comments may have been confirmation to William that he had made a good choice. Then she thought,

"I hope these people know that I am so much deeper than all of that. I hope William knows that too!"

Lyla realized that she had been lost in William's world now for several days. She noticed how she could probably lose her identity quickly in this large world of the Lord William T. Jenson. Suddenly she was not Lyla Jane Wilson anymore. Suddenly she was William's new friend or even William's new wife. When she would let her mind run along those thoughts, a weird feeling would come over her. She was a woman of the 2000's. She was liberated. She was no one's little woman. (If) and she said (If) sometime in the future she ever did hope to marry or try it all again she would want to be someone's equal. She would never want to be that rib that was taken from some man somewhere and give up all rights of her own.

In this respect the south worried Lyla. Even though she had spent many years of her life in the south, she had never had to deal with this. She had heard so many stories about those further south or deeper in the south than she. Well, Mississippi is about as *Deep South* as one can get. She could now see how easily things like that could happen. She had only been in this community three days and she noticed quickly how powerful, strong and in control the Mr. William T. Jenson was. She was very sure he had been raised as a perfect *Southern*

Gentleman and he would expect his woman to be the perfect *Southern Bell*.

Lyla snapped back into reality and realized that even with her fears that she was truly having fun. She loved being babied and cared for by this big strong man. She loved the attention he was giving her and she was going to enjoy the rest of her visit just as she had so far. She was going to consider this a most wonderful vacation. A vacation spent with one of the best looking men she had ever laid eyes upon! A vacation in a mansion upon a plantation, sorry 'ranch', with warm feelings and much happiness! When would a week like this ever come along again? Lyla was very happy that she had come.

The following day, Lyla adorned her Western wear and walked through the barns and stables with William. He was so proud of his beautiful animals. He had what looked like thousands of cattle. He had pets running lose everywhere. A goat came right up to Lyla and ate out of her hand. She could not imagine this. She watched as William tramped through each barn with no regard of debris that lay in his way. Lyla was side stepping any waste that she would come across. William did not seem to notice that there was even any there. He was in his element and he was enjoying telling Lyla all about each and every animal. All seemed to have a story and every one of them had a name.

As the tour continued, the couple spoke to many men and a couple of women that William called his hands. Lyla could not help but wonder what the payout must be on a place like this. She had just passed a long beautiful bunk house, unlike those of her dreams, but with the same necessity. This bunk house was more like an apartment building. It was long and only one floor, but it was plain to see that each party had their own apartment. Doors were lined across the front of the building. Small patios were in front and each had a front door.

They walked until they arrived at one of the largest stables that Lyla had ever seen. The stables, nor the barns could be seen from the beautiful home. As a matter of fact she and William had driven to these barns, bunk house and stables. They seemed to be more than a mile away from the beautiful mansion.

Arriving inside of these pretty stables, Lyla was introduced to William's prized horses. He had just about every kind of a horse a person could own. He had dancing horses. He had very large horses and he had riding horses. He showed Lyla his tack room that was filled with many show pieces. Many had been hand tooled and were made of silver. Lyla was quite impressed. She had always loved horses, but had not ridden one since she was very young. Would she have a fear this day?

The couple walked down the long opening in the center of the stables until they came upon two beautiful quarter horses that were all decked out in their riding gear. The wranglers had prepared two beautiful horses for the couple's afternoon ride. Lyla did not have to ask which horse she was to ride because the smaller horse was all decked out in pink. She wanted to impress her host with her knowledge of horses and thankfully the horse she was about to ride was

162

smarter than she. She was able to pull herself up onto the horse without any loss of limbs or pride.

Lyla realized that her handsome stranger was aware that she was not that knowledgeable about the horses, because he was ever so attentive and watching her every move from the corner of his eyes. As they were leaving the stables, William's horse took off in a mild run. Her horse followed the same pattern. Lyla was not prepared for this, but she hang on very tightly. William slowed his horse and dropped back alongside of her. He said,

"You may want to press down on your feet and raise your body somewhat when your horse trots or canters. If you don't and you let your butt bounce up and down on that saddle, you will hurt tomorrow!"

Lyla did not know what canter meant but she was not about to ask at this minute. She assumed it meant something about a running horse. Every fiber of her brain and body was concentrated upon just staying on this wild animal. Even with all of her fear she chuckled at her thoughts. She knew that William would laugh if she called his beautiful, what she supposed they called calm horse a wild animal. She was nervous none-the-less.

After the long ride across a very long meadow, Lyla began to get more comfortable. William was walking his horse in a slow pace and her horse seemed to just follow the commands of the other horse. She was starting to feel safer. As she looked out over the miles and miles of beautiful property she felt once more that she was in some sort of a movie or possibly a dream. She reminded herself to pinch herself but she felt she could not let go of some of her grip upon the reins

163

of the horse. Yes, this whole trip was making her feel as though she may be in some sort of a dream or a vision. She had never seen a more beautiful place. She had never been with a more handsome man. She had never met anyone who seemed to have or own more than this man owned.

How could Lyla be sure that she was not just dreaming? Things like this just do not happen to an aging woman. Most men who are rich, who live like William and who are drop dead gorgeous such as he, go for the young eye candy type women who they can carry around on their arm. It would not matter if these type men were ninety. They could still attract those women because of their wealth. What did William want with her? She scolded herself for being silly and rode alongside peacefully while her handsome stranger was watching her every move. Then she had a sweet thought when she thought of how maybe, just maybe William had more depth than that. Maybe he preferred to be with someone whom he felt that he had something in common with. Maybe he preferred a woman who was at least old enough to be his children's mother. She always wanted people to know that she had depth. Why was she second guessing William? Obviously he had values and hopes as well!

The couple rode along the pretty fields for at least an hour. They were coming upon a forest ahead. The pretty trees as a backdrop behind the secluded meadow made for a picture that one would only see in books. Lyla watched as her handsome host jumped down from his large horse in a way that was as if he were only stepping down the steps in his home. He moved with such ease to where Lyla was concerned as to how gracefully she was going to be while getting off of her horse. This was not a worry she had to ponder on long because William walked over to her, reached up and put his arm around her waist. He lifted her and sat her down upon the ground. She was always amazed at how William could pick her up as if she were a feather and move her all about with no effort. She smiled at him and said,

"Thank you, kind sir!"
He reached down and pecked her upon her lips with his lips as he said,

"You are quite welcome, pretty lady!"

Lyla was so surprised at herself for not asking questions. This was so unlike her. She was just following the lead of this handsome stranger. He obviously had planned a wonderful week for her and she was obviously enjoying it very much.

As William lead the way to a knoll, Lyla could see that it overlooked a brisk brook flowing from inside of the woods. William had brought along a large sort of tote bag looking thing that had been tied and hung on both sides behind his saddle, but now he had it hanging over one of his large shoulders. This was like shoulder bags for a horse she would guess. After walking to what she was sure he thought to be the perfect place, he laid it upon the ground and unfastened the latches. First he pulled out a blanket. Next he pulled out a tablecloth. Then she was so amazed when she saw a bottle of wine come out of that tote package. She was even more amazed when a wedge of cheese and crackers were placed upon the small tablecloth. Her handsome host never missed a thing. She wondered if he was always such a gallant host.

Even with all of the town's people reassurances, Lyla's second thought was, she wondered just how many other women this amazing man had brought to this very spot. Maybe the town's people just didn't know. Maybe it did not matter. Maybe she should just enjoy herself instead of finding herself jealous of any woman who had ever had the company of this wonderful man.

Chapter 12

The rest of the week was wonderful for the now totally relaxed Lyla. She could not remember ever having a vacation such as this. She felt she had walked into a book. This week felt like a romance novel while she watched the movie play out in front of her very eyes. William and his place were all too good to be true. No one could live like this. No one could have as little of problems as this big wonderful man seemed to have. Lyla laughed as she thought,

"Okay lady, when you dream, you *do* dream big!"

Once again she said to herself,

"Since you are able to conjure up a two hundred year old slave girl, surely you can conjure up a man like William! This cannot be real. This has got to all be just a dream!"

Lyla pinched herself over and over again and of course she realized that she was in reality at The Jenson Ranch. No she was not dreaming. No she was not losing her mind. Well maybe that could be debatable, but she was really there with the man of her dreams. She knew that she must grasp reality on another realm. She must be rational. Why would this man want anything to do with her? She was sure there would be plenty of ladies of his stature and station in life right here in his own community. She had seen other such homes on her trip to William's house on that last road they took from town. Obviously this was a very wealthy community. There was most probably a long line of broken hearts in this very place. Lyla could vision them all left broken hearted and lying about while missing the ever handsome Lord William T. Jenson.

What about William's ex-wife or wives? She knew so little. She had now found that one had died and he was considered a widower the same as she was a widow. But the one or more living brought questions to Lyla's mind. William was not forthcoming with this information. Why would any of those from the past have let this man get away? Why did he seem intent on having her? She was from miles and miles away. She was from a working class people. She laughed at that thought, because she knew that William worked as well. Where did those terms come from anyway? A working class! Most everyone worked in one way or another. Even the richest of men worked hard to either get more money or to keep what they had acquired.

The ideas about any ex-wives or girlfriends would haunt Miss Lyla on her plane ride home. She had been given such a wonderful gift while being allowed to see into her handsome stranger's lifestyle. She had been given such a wonderful vacation. Why must she pick everything apart into tiny pieces? Was she that insecure? Even though William acted as though he enjoyed her visit as much as she, she could not help but wonder what this week had meant to him. She knew now that she must put her feelings upon a shelf in their proper place and guard herself from falling deeper in love. That would be a tragedy, because she was very sure that a permanent relationship would never work. She and her handsome stranger were from two totally different worlds.

As Lyla reflected upon the beautiful week spent in Mississippi, she wondered at many things. One oddity was that a maid had placed her western clothing in that large armoire. She had cleaned them and then zipped each item up in a dust free cover. Lyla took this to mean that they must not be hers. This made her a bit mad, so she asked William why the maid would do this. He bluntly said,

"Because I told her to! I will buy you more of the same for your next trips here! That is now your closet and you may leave whatever you wish up there. Please make yourself at home. I imagined you would not have a need for those kinds of clothing in that other world!"

Lyla knew this to be true, but she was not sure how to react with these kinds of remarks. William had taken complete charge and he was expecting her to come back to this wonderful place, and often! Why would she fight something like that? She loved his home. She loved the ranch. She loved him! Oh Dear God, had she just said what she thought she said? Was it too late for her? Was she too deeply in love with the Lord William T. Jenson to turn back now?

Once Lyla made it safely home, she found that her mother was not doing well. She was happy that she had arrived at the time that she did. She drove her mother to a doctor. The doctor quickly put her into a hospital. Lyla now felt selfish and guilty for not being there when her mother was not feeling well. She waited in the doctor's office for his official word. Finally he walked into the office while holding her mother's chart. He started his conversation by saying,

"She should not be alone. I realize that you, as many family members do, want to keep your mother at home. I do not see how that is going to be possible much longer. She needs to be placed into a nursing home!"

Lyla was shocked. She had asked a neighbor to sit with her mother while she was off in Mississippi. She had never been completely alone. Yes, she tried hard to do the right thing for her mother. Now the doctor was telling her that she would have to send her away!

Lyla stayed at the hospital with her mother until late hours that night. She read to her from the newspaper. They watched TV and she tried to get food into her mother's frail body. The woman was not hungry. She was most usually a very cheerful lady, so she would not let her weakness or her needs show any more than she had too. Lyla finally went home. On the drive home, she turned her cell phone back on. There were several calls from William. So, once she walked into the door, she phoned him. He had been worried when he could not reach her. She told him what was going on. Then she told him what the doctor had said to her. When she shared this information, she cried. She was at her wits end. What was she to do? The comfort of telling William all of her problems put her in a comfort zone and she had poured her heart out to him. He got very quiet. Lyla said,

"I am sorry I lost it there and bent your ear with my problems. Please forgive me!"

Instead of saying okay and going on with another conversation, he said,

"Would you like for me to come out there to be with you?"

Lyla thanked him for his concern and said,

"No, I'll be alright!"

But she was not alright. She was stressed and she was worried sick.

In the following days Lyla was to learn that the doctors were not going to release her mother to her care at the end of her hospital stay. The only way that they would do that was if Lyla could afford a hospital bed, a full duty nursing staff and monitors of all kinds. What was she to do? She had promised her mother that as long as she was alive, she would never have to go to a nursing home.

After her mother had been in the hospital for four days, Lyla knew that she had to make some hard decisions. She must check out the nursing homes in her area. She had spoken with her mother. Her mother had told her that she knew that she had to do what she had to do. On Wednesday night she had talked in length with William about her situation. She was so thankful to have him to lean upon. He wanted to help in any way that he could. Suddenly he said,

"Lyla, I have the perfect solution. You have nothing there but a low paying job. Why don't you and your mother come and live with me? You know that I have this huge house. I have waiters. I have cooks who know how to cook the right kinds of food for your mother. The doctors could give them guidance and I *DO* have the funds for the around the clock nurses they say that she needs."

Then he said as if an afterthought,

"Yes, that is the solution. Tell your boss that you quit. We can take care of your home and belongings. I will send someone to pack you and your mother's things. Tell her doctor to contact a doctor here and all will be taken care of. We can

171

fly your mother here in a special type plane that is designed for that sort of thing. Besides, I would love to meet your precious mother! Mine has been gone too many years now. I will enjoy having her here."

Then as if she had no say in the matter what so ever, he said,

"Well, it is all settled then. I will get to work on this end the very first thing in the morning."

Lyla sat there in shock. Did this man handle everything in his life this way? Snap decisions seemed to be his forte`. His money made these sorts of things easier for him she would guess, but an outlook on life in his way was most unusual to Lyla. This large and in charge man just made a decision. He never even asked for Lyla's opinion. Lyla was not so sure that she liked this kind of behavior, but she felt guilty for feeling the least bit of resentment when this wonderful man was offering so much. What a wonderful gift that he was willing to give. He was also very right! He did have a wonderful solution. She would be able to keep her mother from going to a nursing home! But, how could she expect him to do this for her and her mother?

Lyla lay awake for hours wondering what she was to do. She did not want to ask William to take care of her and her mother. She did not want to move her mother light years away from her home. She did not want to take these things from William, but she knew she had to think of her mother first. She did not want her mother wasting away in an old nursing home. She had made her a promise. She also knew that if they placed her mother where she could look out over the beautiful ranch and gardens, she would truly enjoy the rest of her days. So, finally before she went to sleep, she consoled herself by saying she would have a long talk with her mother tomorrow.

Lyla's mother was just as sharp as she had always been. She would often say,

"I'm still sixteen inside. Only my body got old!"

The following morning the talk that was needed so badly was started by Lyla. She could see the dismay when she told her mother that the doctors would not let her care for her by herself. She knew that her mother had accepted the fact that she must go to a nursing home. She could see the hurt and the pain of this idea in her precious mother's eyes. Then Lyla laid before her the other scenario. Her mother's eyes got wide and she asked,

"Why would that man want to do that?"
She answered by saying,

"I think he is in love with me mother!"
Her mother's eyes clouded over when she asked,

"How do you feel about him Honey?"
She thought a minute. Then she said,

"Mother, I believe I am in love with him too. I have just been afraid to dream. I felt there would never be a way that we could be together. We came from two different worlds."
Her mother said,

"That is what I wanted to hear! Did you ever think that God may have put me in this way so that you two could be together! I have never wanted to be a burden to anyone. Now it sounds as though I would be a burden to your young man!"

Lyla said,

"Oh no mother, you do not understand. This man is very, very rich. He is richer than anyone I have ever known. He has servants who care for ever room of the house. I don't know for sure, but I would say there are about forty rooms in that house. Mother, it is an old Southern Mansion with beautiful gardens and terraces. I just know you would love that place. Also, the young man, as you called him, would never be troubled in any way. He could live there without even knowing you are there. Of course I know that is not what he wants to do. He stated that he had longed to meet my precious mother."

Lyla saw a nice smile come over her mother's face when she laughed and said,

"Alright then Lyla, I would love to live in Mississippi!"

Now Lyla must get very busy. She had so much to take care of before the release of her mother. The following week, Lyla and William stayed on the phone preparing the large move. Lyla never imagined that she would be moving to Mississippi. If the thought had ever passed her mind it would be a fleeting one. She believed that to be impossible. She also had believed that hers and William's relationship was impossible. Now everything was happening way too fast. She could not dwell on anything. She had to do as she must for her mother. She knew that. Therefore there were no thoughts about herself. There were no thoughts as to whether she and William were moving too fast. There were no thoughts as to whether this was the right thing for them and their relationship. People did not ordinarily move in together before they had talked over something like marriage or anything else. Of course in this case, Lyla knew that living in that mansion would be the same as living separately if they wished it to be that way.

Arrangements were made. William was wonderful. He and the doctors had scheduled the flight for her mother. He had all the nurses, bed and supplies in place. Lyla's mother seemed to feel better now and she had a smile upon her pretty face once more. She seemed to be quite pleased to be traveling to a faraway state. By now she had spoken with William on the phone and had said that she found her benefactor to be most charming. She had laughed and said,

"Lyla, that young man must be completely crazy about you! Who would ever go to all of this trouble for a woman he has never met. I will forever be grateful. You be sure and tell him that for me. Will you?"
Lyla said,

"Of course I will mother. You will be able to tell him yourself in a couple of days! I am leaving right after the movers go tomorrow night. My flight will put me there early in the morning, therefore I will be at the mansion when you arrive."
With that she told her mother that she needed rest for her long trip. She kissed her on the forehead and said,

"I'll see you there. The doctors have already had me complete everything that is needed here. They said they are going to give you a sedative shortly and I should not be here in the morning because you need your rest for the long trip."

A smile came over her weakened mother's face when she said,

"See you there kid! I love you!"

Everything moved so fast to where there was not time to think about anything. Lyla's mothers and her belongings were all packed within hours and upon a large moving van headed for Mississippi. She looked around to see the large empty rooms and that saddened her. She was leaving her home once more. Her apartment meant nothing, but her mother's home was the home of her childhood and she was saddened. Her mother would never be coming back to this wonderful old place. For all that she knew, she may never come back either.

Then a knock came upon the door. Lyla opened it to find a real-estate dealer. She was taken aback by this appearance. She found that William had phoned the lady and gentleman who were now standing in her mother's living room. She was shocked and mad at first when she realized that she and William had not spoken about selling the house. Of course in this time of crisis, they had not spoken of much of anything but the urgent needs at hand. Him being a completely in control gentleman, Lyla finally realized that he would have thought that this was the most logical thing to do. Her mother was never coming back. She knew in her heart that she was never coming back either. What would be left to come back to? Thankfully William had been compassionate enough to realize that she and her mother would want their life long belongings close to them, so he had made arrangements for all of these things to go to Mississippi.

Under different circumstances, Lyla knew that she would have been upset with William for taking total charge of her life. In this case she had to be thankful. She could have never managed the things that William was doing for her and her mother. Without him, her mother would be headed for a local nursing home on this very day. She was so very thankful that was not happening. She could not thank William enough. He had stepped up to the plate and taken charge in her time of need. She would be eternally grateful.

Chapter 13

Lyla was hoping that her mother was comfortable as she was standing at the ticket counter of the airport. Like everything else that was happening, Lyla was informed that her reservation had been paid for by the one and only Mr. Jenson. She marveled at the thought of how wonderful it must be to be able to just write a check or just charge anything in the world whenever you wanted. She had never had that luxury. Obviously, William had never done without that luxury. Even so it was still amazing as to the things that he could accomplish in such a short time.

As Lyla sank down into her now first class seat on the plane, she started to reflect. She was amazed as to how life works sometimes. Who would have ever dreamed that she would meet someone like William? Just days ago, who would have ever dreamed that she and her mother would be moving to Mississippi to live with this rich and handsome man? The fast happenings were almost too much for the lady to comprehend. There was simply no time to question whether this was right or wrong. There was no time to debate, research or anything. There was really no time for Lyla to question what she was doing. Maybe that was a good thing because Lyla had the habit of questioning everything to death. All Lyla knew was that this was the best thing for her mother. She could never give her this treatment by herself. Besides, she also knew that she was becoming quite fond of the handsome Mr. Jenson. Only problem being, she wished they had been given the time to become more acquainted before moving in together. However, this did not seem to trouble

William one bit, but it was happening so fast to where Lyla was kind of crazy.

Lyla had never seen a double rainbow before. Just the few days ago after a rain and just as she was turning from one road onto another, she saw the most beautiful double rainbow. She considered this to be a sign from God that 'YES' everything is going to be just fine and 'YES' she and her mother were supposed to move to Mississippi. This may sound a little shallow to a normal person, but with the things that happened to Lyla, there was absolutely nothing strange about that. She no longer considered herself to be normal in anyway and she knew in her heart that this rainbow was a sign.

Although the flight was not to be all that long of a flight, Lyla knew that they would be stopping in Dallas. She also knew that she did not have to leave the plane because the same plane would be going on to her destination. Therefore she relaxed. She had never flown first class before and she loved the luxury of it all. The seats were wide and so very comfortable. The pressure of the days that had just passed made it feel as if it had been months since her carefree visit with William. In reality, it had only been three weeks. Here she was again, heading back to that wonderful place. The difference being now was that this time she was going to her new home. Wow! How did all of this happen? Who could have ever believed that this actually could be happening? Life was moving way too fast for the conservative Lyla!

The poor woman was exhausted. The flight attendant had asked her what she could get for her.

She asked for a pillow. Within seconds she was asleep. Suddenly she was dreaming. She was in Flossy Mae's body once more. She was coherent enough to think,

"Not now Flossy Mae! I have too much on my plate right now. Please leave me in my world for a while!"

It was as if Flossy Mae did not hear her request. Her Flossy Mae entity was sitting on the corner of her bed and crying uncontrollably. She had her apron up in her hands and was using it to wipe away her tears. Suddenly, two taps came upon the door. Then the Colonel Winthrop Wayne walked in. He latched the door behind him and then he sat down on the bed beside of Flossy Mae. He started to talk. He said,

"Flossy Mae, what is the matter with you?"

She could not talk. She was shaking all over. The large man put out his arm and brought her body close to his. Then in a softer voice he said,

"Flossy Mae you are going to have to tell me what it is!"

She finally got a voice and whimpered,

"It's Jenny! It is Jenny!"

Jenny was their eleven year old daughter. Of course no one on the plantation knew that Jenny was the Colonel's daughter. However, by now some people were questioning these facts. The Colonel was just so powerful to where no one would ever speak out about their doubts. Jenny, as were the others, was of a very light skin color. She was a beautiful little girl. Other than her faded color, she looked just like her mother. The Colonel said,

"Where is she? Where is she Flossy Mae?"

She said,

"She ran out of here like lightening and ran straight to the first barn."

The Colonel jumped up and rushed out of the door. He shut the bedroom door hard. He was aggravated with Flossy Mae because she could not seem to get out what had happened. All he knew was that something was terribly wrong. Flossy Mae could not stop crying long enough to tell him what his daughter's problem was.

Colonel Wayne marched to the barn as if he were on the battlefield. He rushed past all of the buildings and the trees along the way. He threw open the big doors and screamed,

"Jenny! Jenny, where are you?"
None of the children had ever been told that the Colonel was their father. Oh they knew something was not quite right about their lives. They were treated very wonderful by the standards of the treatment of slaves. They knew that their master had complete control over them and their survival. They knew that the Colonel was in charge of every decision they made. But that was just it, they could make decisions. Other slaves could not! The oldest son had told his mother at one time that he loved the Colonel. He said,

"Mother, do you know that white man treats me as if I am his own son sometimes!"
Flossy Mae had shuddered when she knew that she must keep the secret that Colonel Wayne *was* their father, even from them. The children still knew that he cared very deeply for each one of them. They could feel his love. They had watched the large Colonel crumble at the death of their older brother. They had witnessed many tender

moments between the Colonel and their mother. Some of the older children had wondered about their shade of blackness. Some ask their mother why they were treated so very much differently than the other black children upon the plantation.

On this day it was becoming quite obvious that the Colonel did not care who knew about his children. He had one in trouble and that is all that mattered to him this day. Suddenly a whimper came from high up in the loft. The Colonel jumped upon the ladder and proceeded to climb to where he could hear the sound. Once he found Jenny, he did not have to ask what the problem was. She had blood upon her torn dress. She looked like a wild tiger had gotten a hold of her. The Colonel reached down and swept the little girl up into his arms. He held her close and he felt tears coming up behind his eyelids. He rubbed her hair from her face and told her to look at him. She did, but she could not stop crying. He said,

"Tell me Jenny who did this to you? You have to tell me who did this to you."
She said that she did not know his name, but that he was white!

Now the Colonel racked his brain. Who had been at his plantation this day? Who had been able to roam around the plantation long enough to do this to his eleven year old daughter? He knew that any of his help would have never done such a thing. They would have believed that the Colonel would kill them if they did. He also believed that his men were of better standards than that. Then he was able to narrow it down to two men. Two men by the names of Bo and Watts had delivered grain to the grain bins this morning. He had noticed that they lingered there much too long and he had wondered as to why. Now he knew.

The Colonel carried the little girl into the house. He took her straight to her mother's room. Once more he latched the door behind them. He said to Flossy Mae for her to wash Jenny up and put fresh clothing on her. She did just as he asked. Then he took the little girl by the hand and walked out of the door. Flossy Mae was worried as to what may happen next. She thought as she stared into his eyes that she had seen murder in the big Colonel this day. She knew someone was going to pay. Someone may even die! She had never seen that look in the Colonel's eyes before! She could see flames coming from directly inside of his pupils.

The Colonel put Jenny high upon a wagon seat. He hooked up the horses and started across the plantation to where some of his help was working. He hollered for those in his employee to come with him and he loaded them on the wagon as well, while leaving the slaves to work on their own. They were off to the neighboring village. The Colonel explained a little on his way to the white gentleman whom he had with him. He told them that he had a score to settle. He said,

"You boys may not like this score that I have to settle because it is with a white man! He has done something to me and my family that is unforgivable."
Then he said,

"I swear to you, as God be my witness, that man will walk through the gates of Hell this very day!"

It became apparent that the Colonel could care less at this point if anyone knew or did not know that Jenny was his daughter. If they did not already know, all of these men had to guess the answer to that question on this fateful day. Then the Colonel looked each man in the face and said,

"Do I have your support?"

Many of these men had fought right alongside of the Colonel during the wars. They had come home with him to work under his employment. They were as loyal to the man as they were during battle. The men just hung their heads for a while; then one of them said,

"We're with you Colonel. We are all with you!"

Upon arrival into this small village, the group pulled in front of a mill that was along the river. The Colonel jumped down and went inside. He came back to the wagon and said,

"We have a wait boys!"

Within the hour another wagon pulled up in front of the mill. There were two men sitting on the bench seat on the front of the wagon. The Colonel motioned for his men to get down from their wagon and they marched over to the other. The Colonel spoke and said,

"Have either of you ever seen the little girl who is sitting upon my wagon before?"

They laughed as if that was some kind of a dumb question. One of them said,

"If you've seen one wench, you have seen 'em all!'

With that statement the Colonel walked over and picked up the small child from the wagon. Everyone looked at him in shock. The two men had no idea why this large man would be carrying one of his slaves in that manner. He spoke in a loud controlling voice, when he said,

"Jenny, have you seen either of these men today?"

The little girl said yes and buried her tear filled eyes into the Colonel's shoulder. He got even louder and said,

"Jenny, did one of these men hurt you today?"

Jenny said,

"Yes Sir!"

All of the men stood steadily behind the large Colonel when he asked,

"Which one Jenny? Which one hurt you?"

The little girl pointed to the large man they called Bo. With that remark the Colonel gently placed the little girl back upon the wagon and he took out his sword. Now the puzzled man said,

"You came all of this way over here after me because I did something to one of your little wenches? You are crazy man! She is just a wench!"

Then the belligerent man said the words that set the Colonel on fire and pushed him to have even more murder on his brain this day, when he said,

"You are just mad because I got to her before you did."

With that remark the man Bo took his fist and tried to hit the Colonel. The Colonel grabbed his arm with great force and gave him a thundering blow with his other hand. His fist hit the man in his temple so hard to where a normal man would have been dead. The strong man Bo came right back at the Colonel. By now the other men were all surrounding the two fighting men! The man Watts backed off and said,

"I have no idea what happened. Yes, I was at your plantation earlier, but I was busy filling your bins Sir!"

The Colonel had fire coming from his eyes and his fist drawn back to plaster the man Watts straight in the face when he asked,

"Do you know what your partner did?"

He looked the Colonel straight in the eyes and said,

"No Sir, I don't! As I said before, I was filling the bins!"

Somehow the Colonel realized that this man was telling the truth. He motioned to his employees to reach in the wagon to get some rope. Everyone's eyes got big. They were of the belief that the Colonel was going to string this man up right there in the middle of town. Instead he told his men to tie the man Bo around his feet and his hands. They did as he asked. They tied his feet and hands together. They threw him, with a large thud sound, into the wagon. His head hit the hard wood floor with a bang.

The workers and the Colonel said nothing on the trip back to the plantation. The man on the floor was begging for his life. He was rambling on and on about how he had only messed with a little wench. By now another man was driving the wagon. The Colonel was holding tightly onto this man. The man realized that he was getting nowhere with his begging, so he became belligerent again and he said,

"Do with me what you please, but that little wench was good. Sorry you missed out on her first go around. But she sure was good. She was very good! I would do it again in a heartbeat!"

Never had the Colonel used so much force as he did when he took his hard soled boot and crashed it down upon the man Bo's face. The blood went everywhere. He started to bleed uncontrollably.

As the group pulled up the long driveway and arrived in front of the house, the Colonel said he would be right back. He took his daughter into the house and left her with her mother. He ran back out of the house while Flossy Mae watched out of the window. She feared for what was going to happen next. She had never in all of her years seen the Colonel as mad as he was this day.

The large Colonel jumped back upon the wagon and the group took off towards the woods. Flossy Mae knew in her heart that a man was going to die this day. Flossy Mae did not want Lyla to think the worst of the Colonel so she told her that in their day, justice was always carried out by the land owners. There was most likely a vote before a hanging, but this is just the way things were done during those times. Courts were almost an unknown factor in their parts. Flossy Mae felt sad for the man even though she knew what he had done to her daughter. She felt sad for her daughter, her family and the Colonel. She felt sad about life! She wondered,

"Why did it all have to be this way? Why did life have to be so hard? Why? Why did it have to be so very hurtful?"

The airplane hit the runway with a jolt. Lyla was awakened. She looked out of the window while she had a talk with herself, Flossy Mae or her soul. She was not quite sure which. She thought,

"Why are you showing me all of this today Flossy Mae? I know that had to be absolutely terrible. I am so sorry you had to go through all of that. My heart bleeds for Jenny. Thankfully the Colonel took control and protected you and the children as much as he could. He must have been a very caring gentleman, even with the ways of your times. I just don't understand why you would tell me all of this at this time. I am so covered up with worries of my own. There is so much on my plate. I am praying that I am not making the biggest mistake of my life. I am trying to do what is right for my mother."

Then she thought that maybe she was too harsh with Flossy Mae, only to laugh out loud when she thought of how crazy that she must surely be. She thought,

"That is just purely stupid and very crazy lady. You are Flossy Mae!"

With that thought she reached in front of her and picked up a magazine. She would be stuck at this airport for a while, so she might as well be comfortable.

Lyla watched while many other passengers disembarked and as the new ones loaded on the plane. Dallas sun was shining through her window on this pretty day and she was completely engrossed in her thoughts of the move. Suddenly she ask the same question that her mother had ask,

"Why would William be willing to do all of this?"

They had not been seeing each other all that long. Common sense would tell anyone that this couple had a long way to go before one could call them a permanent relationship. Gee! She had only been to his home one time before and visits to her home state were far and in between. Yet, they did have closeness, warmth and a home feeling unlike anything that Lyla had ever felt before. What was that all about? She was only to wonder!

While Lyla and her plane were on the ground, she picked up the phone and she called William. He was happy to hear from her. Out of his mouth in a blaze, just like everything else he said and done in his life, the big rambunctious man chimed in with,

"What's your mother's favorite color?"
She answered in amazement,

"Yellow! Why do you ask?"
William did what he does way too often. He changed the subject and told her he was anxious for her arrival. He told her that he would be at the airport. Then he dolefully said,

"By the way, we are having roast beef for dinner!"
Lyla laughed. She was always amazed at the spirit of this man. He was so happy go lucky about just about everything. She knew that the big man loved to eat, but concerned about dinner? Lyla had to laugh. She was amazed as to how the trauma with her and her mother had not fazed this man. Life was going on as usual. Or, just like she and her mother had been there forever. She did not quite understand the lack of adjustment time with this most unusual man. She felt a shock factor as to how he acted as though this was just his family and he was doing his duties of taking care of them. But, she loved him for doing what he was doing just the same. She was also very happy that he seemed to be happy about it all.

Finally the plane landed once more. This time it landed in Mississippi. As Lyla walked through the tunnel she could see William standing at the very opening. Just as she stepped onto the solid floor, the large man picked her up and swung her all around. He said in a loud blusteriest voice,

"Gee, it is good to see you! I missed you!" Lyla looked around to see if she should be embarrassed. After all they were not teenagers. They were older people who probably should act their age. But she also realized that William did not care what other people thought and thanks to William, she was starting to feel the very same way about life. It was way too short anyway. Why not enjoy it. She had always been way too uptight and she knew it.

Lyla laughed and said,

"But-t-t Lord William, I have only been gone a week or two. Maybe three!!"
He placed a kiss upon her lips and said,

"But-t-t Miss Lyla, you are home now!"
She stood there for a minute while she realized this to be true. My God, this was true! She, her mother, lock stock and barrel was now in Mississippi to stay. This had to all soak in. Lord what a move! What a quick move! Lyla had to wonder as to how this story would end. Right now she was just happy to be on the ground. She knew she must get her mother situated and happy.

The couple rushed to the ranch. William took Lyla straight to the room that had been prepared for her mother. It was only a few doors down the hall from the room everyone called Lyla's room at this time. As the big double doors were opened by William, Lyla was in awe! She could not believe her eyes. She cried with happiness. William took her into his arms and said,

"You approve then?"

She laughed and said,

"Lord yes, I approve. How on earth did you do all of this with such a short notice?"

There before her was a large, full sized hospital bed. It did not look like a hospital bed. It had a pretty brass head board, nice pillows and a pretty yellow bedspread. One could see the adjustment buttons and the lifts on the side, but one had to look hard to see them. This was a most beautiful bed. Across the wall was another armoire similar to the one in Lyla's room. It was already filled with her mother's clothing. The silk lined doors were standing open as if to welcome its new owner. Beside the bed was an old rocking chair that belonged to her mother and had been handed down to her by her grandmother. A dressing table had been filled with all of her mother's belongings. Her hats and scarves had been placed ever so neatly upon pretty brass hooks that stuck out from the walls at each side of the dressing table. Many of her mother's whatnots were sitting about. Her pictures from her bedroom back home were hanging upon the walls. Tables and shelves around the room were covered with her children and grandchildren's pictures. They walked into the wonderful bathroom where all of her mother's toiletries were sitting about. Lyla was so elated.

She reached over and pulled William close to her and said,

"You Sir are unbelievable. I don't believe that you are real. You are so amazing. I thank you so very much. I thank you with all of my heart."
Then she broke down and cried all over his shirt while he held her close. He said,

"I'm glad you like it. I hope you mother does too."
She laughed with her mouth wide open and said,

"Lord, she is going to love it!"
Then William said,

"I chose this room because it has a walk in shower. I purchased her a rust proof wheelchair where she can wheel it right into the shower and it will not rust. Once she locks down the wheels, she will feel the freedom of taking a bath by herself. I know that would be important to me should I be in her condition."

Lyla could not believe this man. Could he even be real? Was she really not dreaming? Just as that thought crossed her mind she felt the warmness of a big hand that had reached out and was leading her to the terrace. The French doors opened and they were standing out in the open air. The view was the same wonderful view that Lyla enjoyed from her lovely room. She knew that her mother would absolutely love her surroundings. She was happy that she could provide this for her mother. Then she thought, actually, I am happy that William *would* provide this for my mother.

The mother was to arrive within hours so William knew that Lyla must have a lot to do before her arrival. So, he said,

"I'll leave you alone for a while honey. I know you want to prepare for your mother."
Lyla said,

"Well, it looks like you have just about completed everything that needs done."

William walked out and said that he would see her in a while.

Lyla looked her mother's room over more, arranged a drawer or two in the way she knew that her mother would want her privates and things. Then she headed for her own room. She was in bad need of freshening up. Besides, she must unpack all of her belongings. She was moving also. Yes! Good Lord, she was moving into this mansion. How on earth did that come about?

Just three weeks ago Lyla was standing at the door of this very room in amazement and surprise for the very first view. Three weeks ago she was telling herself she and William could never have a future because they came from two totally different worlds. Three weeks ago she spent the most wonderful week of her life upon a ranch of a wonderful friend, knowing that was all they could ever be, considering they lived in two different parts of the country. Today, she was moving into this fairytale with plans of never leaving. She climbed up on the high bed and sank down into its comfort and said,

"You are one lucky lady Miss Lyla! I don't know how, but you became one lucky little girl!" Quickly she bounced back off the bed. She knew that she had far too much to do to let herself think or to drift off into a sleeping place at this time. Thinking too much about this would probably drive her over the edge anyway, so she resolved herself to just think about it all tomorrow!

Chapter 14

The ambulance drove up the large circle driveway and stopped directly in front of the house. Lyla ran out to greet her mother. Many servants walked alongside her to fulfill their duties. As they rolled the loving mother out of the car, Lyla could see her wide, bright eyes. She hollered,

"Well mother, what do you think?"

Her mother got tears of joy in her eyes and said, "It is beautiful baby. It is just beautiful. Lyla looked around and she saw William coming down the steps. She called for him and he walked up to the side of the car and looked down at the ailing woman. Lyla said,

"Mother, this is William!"

The mother looked up at him with a large smile and said,

"You are an angel! I just know you are! A very handsome, beautiful angel at that! I will never be able to repay you for your kindness. I will never be able to thank you enough for what you are doing for me! I will go to my grave appreciating your big heart. I love you for that young man! I am just going to love you for the rest of my days. I hope that is okay with you?"

William laughed as he leaned over and kissed her on the forehead. He said,

"Of course that is okay. I accept your love and I know that I already love you and I am going to love having you here. I want you to know that I only do this sort of thing for beautiful ladies and you certainly are one of those!"

Lyla watched as her mother blushed, she smiled and everyone started into the house.

Lyla's mother was taken to her room. She had the same reaction that Lyla had only hours ago. She cried when she saw her room. She just stared at it for a while. One of the servants asked her if she found everything satisfactory and if it was okay to push her on into the room. Then and only then did she respond to anyone. She looked at Lyla. Then she looked at William and said,

"My God, I do not think I have ever seen such a beautiful room. Are you sure you want to put a sick old woman like me in there?"
William assured her that this was what he wanted and that this was indeed her room. He told her that if there was anything she needed that was not provided for her by the others, to please let him know and he would rectify it quickly. He then said,

"Relax and adjust. This is your home, please accept it as such. I hope you will enjoy it!"
He squeezed Lyla's hand then he walked off down the hall. Lyla looked down at her mother, who said,

"Mighty nice nursing home, wouldn't you say honey?"
Both ladies laughed.

A nurse came into the room and introduced herself. She ask that everyone leave her with the mother for a while. She stated that she had to check her over after the trauma that the trip may have caused her. Other servants and helpers were floating around everywhere. Lyla excused herself and headed to look for William. She was going to have to get used to this house. She kept getting lost down one hall or another. Finally she had to ask a servant where he was. She found William in the study behind his desk. She ran in to thank him once more for everything that he had done for her and her mother. He only smiled and said,

"Lyla, I don't think you know how much I am going to enjoy having your mother here. I already love her. She is one sweet lady, just as I knew she would be. She had you after all, and I am totally blown away by her daughter."

This time Lyla walked over and kissed him on the top of his head and said,

"I'm kind of blown away with you too Lord William!"

He laughed and repeated,

"Lord William, Huh? Now I could get used to that!"

She laughed and said,

"Don't!"

Then on a more serious note she said,

"I see that you have work to do!"

As she noticed all of the papers and files lined up on his desk.

"I'll see that everything is okay with mother, unpack and then I am going to take a bath. See you at dinner!"

William smiled. As she turned to leave, she could feel the heat of his eyes watching her while she left the room.

That night at dinner, Lyla had dressed once more in a flowing gown. She was not sure that this was the standard at this house but she was so thankful that she had made that decision. William was once more dressed in a tux type suit. Lyla had so much to learn. William dressed each and every night for dinner. She thought of how she must take some money out of her savings account, because she was surely going to need some new

197

clothing. Suddenly, she realized that she had not seen her car outside. It was to be carried on a car carrier to the estate. So, she asked William where it was. He smiled and said,

"I sent it to a garage to have it checked out before bringing it home. In the meantime you can drive anything in the garage. There are several small trucks out there and a sports car. The sports car has something wrong with the clutch. I will get it fixed! You would look beautiful in it!"

Lyla was feeling somewhat uncomfortable without the knowledge that her car was close by. She had never been without a car and hoped that hers would be finished soon.

Dinner went wonderfully. Everything was delicious. Rich wonderful wine was served once more while Lyla thought,

"I must see that wine cellar. It must be something to behold!"

She chuckled a little with her thoughts of that, only to have the curious, questioning eyes of William staring at her. This just made her laugh more. He started to laugh with her. Then he said,

"Want to tell me what is so funny?"

She said,

"Oh, I was just thinking of your wine cellar and of how this could be an alcoholic's dream. Then I thought of how you don't really know me. Yet you moved me and my mother, lock, stock and barrel into your beautiful home. We could be mass murders for all that you know!"

William was not laughing. Instead he just glared at her. Dinner was over so he walked around and pulled her seat out so that she could get up. He took her hand in his and said,

"Let us go see that wine cellar!"

The couple walked down several halls until they arrived at a large closed door that looked like it should have been in a castle somewhere. Lyla was about to say that when William said,

"I had this door flown in from Wales. It used to be in a castle that is now completely destroyed."

Lyla was amazed! She was living in a fairytale. If this wasn't a dream and she was finally realizing that it was not, then someone up there was surely smiling down on her right now.

William reached up and got a large key that had a huge ring upon it and he unlocked the door. The couple went down a flight of stairs and arrived in the most massive wine cellar Lyla had ever seen. It had bottles filled with alcohol lining every wall. The bottles went clear to the very high ceiling. She had never seen so many bottles of alcohol in her entire life. She was fascinated. She stood there with bright eyes and in amazement. William only laughed. Then he said,

"As for your other questions at dinner, I am a very good judge of character. Plus, I have people who are constantly checking backgrounds of anyone I do business with."

Lyla did not know whether to be flattered or mad. Do business with? What the Hell was that supposed to mean? Did he think that he was doing some kind of business with her? As of right now, William Jenson had been the only one giving anything financial to this relationship. He had given and given and Lyla was a bit uncomfortable with that.

Rather than asking the question as to what William meant by saying (doing business with), Lyla chose to let it go. She should not question a man who had been so very kind to her and her mother. What was wrong with her tonight? She imagined that she was just tired from all of the happenings that had gone on in the past few days. She also knew that she was doing some adjusting. She did not want to use anyone, just as she would not want anyone to use her.

William was walking amongst the shelves as if he were looking for something. Lyla took a seat around a beautiful solid wood table. It looked as if it were made from a whole, very large tree stump. Actually it looked like it was made from a whole tree! Stools were circling this large table. They too were made from stumps of trees. Each piece had been varnished to a high gloss and they were beautiful.

Finally, William came around the corner of a shelving unit with a bottle in his hand. He grabbed two glasses and sat down at the table with Lyla. He poured the wine, he sipped a taste and then he said,

"Try that, see if you like it!"
He then held up his glass. As the glasses touched, he toasted with,

"May every evening from this day forth be as wonderful as tonight for you and me, my love!"
He then looked over the glass and said,

"I love you Lyla!"
Lyla did not know quite how to react. She knew that she loved him too but was more or less

surprised that he should say that on this night. So, she said,

"Thank you, love!'

That worked and the two chattered about wine for another thirty minutes.

As the couple was walking up the steps, William said,

"You certainly look lovely tonight. Did I neglect to tell you that?"

Lyla looked back at the wonderfully handsome William who was dressed beautifully in his dinner attire and said,

"You look pretty darn wonderful too Mr. Jenson."

She chuckled and said,

"Well, then again, I have never noticed when you didn't look wonderful!"

William seemed to be in a somewhat unusual mood tonight. Instead of acknowledging her statement he said,

"Lyla do you think you will enjoy living here?"

Lyla laughed and said,

"Who wouldn't? This is a paradise. It is so beautiful and so very wonderful. Life around here seems to be a complete party by my standards. I love it here and I am sure I will love it here always."

Opps! What made her say that? No one has spoken of always. She straightened her composure and said,

"I meant as long as you will have us. Thank you so much for letting my mother and I stay with you. You will never know how much we both appreciate this."

William took Lyla into his arms at the top of the stairs right under the arch of that big door casing and held her tight. He lifted her face so that her eyes met his and said,

"I was hoping you would more than just enjoy living here. I am hoping you will make this your permanent home."

The big man dropped to his knees and said,

"I am asking you to marry me Lyla! Will you marry me?"

Lyla felt her legs go weak. She had not thought that far into the future. All she knew at this point was that she thoroughly enjoyed William's company. She knew that she cared about him. Could she call it love? Well she guessed that she could. She knew that she waited patiently by the phone everyday awaiting a call from this fabulous man. She knew that she missed him during long periods of not seeing him. She knew that she had no interest in any other man ever since that first day of meeting her perfect stranger. Yes, she guessed that she knew that she was surely in love. What woman on this great big earth could ever not fall deeply in love with this man? He was every woman's dream come true! But, dear God, things were moving way too fast! Lyla also knew that William was a true Southern gentleman and he would feel it was the only right thing to do should a couple live together. She knew that he believed it would be improper to live together without that wedding ring.

William was starting to loosen his grip around Lyla because she did not speak for so long. He had a bewildered look upon his face. Lyla snapped out of her tortured thoughts and grabbed William's hands tighter. Right now she hated herself for analyzing everything to death. Why was she like that? She had known for a very long time that she was completely wiped out and deeply in love with William. Why the hesitation? Then she said in a calm and sweet voice,

"Yes William, I will marry you!"
A big smile came upon William's face and he rose to his feet and kissed his bride to be.

The two became quiet while they were in their own thoughts. They still had their glasses of wine in their hands. William locked the cellar door and the couple began walking back down the halls and then out of a patio door. William was swinging the bottle of wine in one hand as they walked down a winding path in the gardens. The moon was bright tonight. The stars were out and oh so very lovely. Neither had much to say! They were only enjoying these wonderful moments. Finally, Lyla broke the silence when they stopped under a lantern light. She said,

"Let me see that bottle. I am getting a buzz!'
William laughed and handed her the bottle. She read on it and it said something in French that she could not read, but she could read the numbers 1929. My goodness, this had to be the most expensive wine she had ever tasted. She knew that it was strong and *very, very* expensive! William laughed once more when he said,

"Don't get used to this wine. I only had one bottle of this and I had prepared to use it only on the most special occasion of my life."
With a twinkle in his eyes he said,

"Darling, tonight is the most special occasion of my life!"
Lyla looked into his eyes and for one of the first times she could read what this wonderful man was

thinking and she saw complete love for her. She saw the depth of his soul for the very first time. He had let her in. She saw complete love. She saw happiness. She replied with,

"Thank you William. This is the most special occasion of my life as well. I love you! I love you with all of my heart!"

The couple finished the rest of the bottle of wine in the gardens and then headed for the house. William said,

"The moon is beautiful tonight. Why don't we go change clothes and go for a ride. I love to trail ride in a full moon. I think you will too."
Lyla laughed as she wondered how she could manage a horse with the buzz she seemed to have at this minute. She said to William,

"Is there any kind of driving rules with horses? Can I get a D.U.I.?"
William broke out in a strong laughter. Lyla loved his strong laugh. It took him a while to regain his composure when he said,

"Sorry, I don't think that applies to horses. I want you to know that I would not put you on a horse that I was not sure about. I would be sure that it knew what it was doing. Ally knows to follow me and she knows how to take care of her rider. He laughed and then added,

"Even if her rider is a bit tipsy!"
Lyla giggled and agreed to go. Then she started wondering if these sorts of things were so very normal around this household. It seemed that everything was on the spare of the moment with the Lord of this house. Everything seemed to

always be just to have fun. She looked at William and said,

"Let me get dressed and then check on mother and I will meet you in the foyer."
William agreed, and she went upstairs to change. She must have taken awhile because when she was finished dressing and walked down the hall to her mother's room she could hear voices inside of the room. She knocked and went in only to find William sitting in the old rocking chair. He had pulled it up close to her mother's bed. He was reading some verses out of the Bible to her mother. Lyla was pleasantly pleased.

The couple stayed with her mother for a while. Lyla could tell that her mother was extremely happy to be where she was. She smiled all of the time. She acted as though she was feeling so much better too. She had been able to move herself from her bed to the wheelchair on two or three different occasions now and told of how she loved to go out on the terrace and look at the beautiful gardens. Lyla was always in amazement over the big man in her life. She was always surprised at his actions. Seemingly, and thankfully she was always pleasantly surprised! William was just too good to be true. Just as the two were about the leave the room, Lyla turned around and said,

"Mother, we have something to tell you!"
Her mother's dark eyes widened as she stared at the handsome couple. Lyla said,

"Mother, William asked me to marry him tonight!"
A big smile came over her mother's face when she said,

"I know. He came to visit me earlier today to ask for my permission and my blessing. I knew he was going to ask you tonight and I could not be happier! We're going to be a family. I love your young man Lyla. He is wonderful!"

Lyla did not know what to think. Her William was always so full of surprises. Now he was getting ready to pull another one on her. He said,

"I guess the proper thing to do now, would be to have you meet my children! I want to meet your children soon too. I have invited mine to dinner Friday night so everyone can meet everyone! Sound okay to you?"

Had Lyla been more sober she knew that all of this would have unnerved her. She wondered if William ever intended to include her feelings in matters that included her before he made any of these snap decisions. Had she been sober she is sure that this invite would have made her almost mad. He was forever saying things after the fact like,

"Is that okay with you? Or I hope that is okay with you!"

What would she do if it wasn't? The deed was always already done. Even in this mellow mood of the evening, Lyla was wondering if she could get used to that, but she contained enough composure to answer William's question when she murmured a shallow,

"Yes!"

After the couple arrived at the stables, Lyla was once more surprised that their horses were already saddled and ready for their ride. What on earth goes on around here? Is she not expected to do anything? A better question was,

"Does William do anything?"

Guess not, maybe that is what is meant by the have it all's and the working class. Maybe saddling a horse was considered manual labor. This must be the ways of the very rich, but it was going to take some adjustment for Lyla. She knew that she would have to get used to this way of life. Then in her funny state of mind tonight she thought,

"When it all comes crumbling down around you lady, I hope you are not so spoiled that you would not know how to take care of yourself anymore."

Lyla snapped back into reality and William helped her get up onto her horse. A strange thought crossed her mind when she thought.

"It is a wonder he does not hire someone to do this!"

Lyla did not like her flippant thoughts and she scolded herself for them. She did, thankfully, have time to reflect on the long ride. Both she and William seemed to stay very quiet. She did ride close to William and she told him that she thought a moonlight ride was very beautiful. As they rode along, Lyla started to take a count of her life. Everything was moving so very fast. Was it moving too fast? She realized that she had in fact fallen very deeply in love with this handsome rancher. The same answers kept coming up. She would repeat and repeat to herself,

"What woman would not fall in love with this man? He was every woman's dream."

Lyla realized that this was the most wonderful opportunity for her ailing mother. She realized that living with William could be nothing but Heaven. Why did she have to analyze everything so thoroughly in her life? Life was short. Why could she not just go with the flow and accept things as they came along? Lord, she was

207

so lucky at meeting William. How many women met a man like this in their whole lifetime? Then she analyzed herself and figured out something that she already knew deep inside. She was just too rigid. She wished that she could make snap decisions just as William could do. She told herself that analyzing everything as she did only made for unhappy. There was no room for unhappy in this world. She was going to be very happy. She was happy with William.

So, the worrying little Miss Lyla decided to leave her worries behind. She knew that she had been given a wonderful opportunity and she valued that. She decided to not let herself stand in the way of her own happiness. Therefore, this was going to be the last time that she was going to question anything to do about marrying her Lord William T. Jenson. She did not care if it was too soon. She did not care if they really knew each other or not. It was settled! She was happy! She knew in her heart that she was going to be very happy!

Chapter 15

Friday night finally came! There had been a whole week of worry on Lyla's part. What if William's children had a problem with Lyla? She knew that they would believe the marriage idea was way too soon. Of course that was based on the fact as to whether William had intentions of telling his children just yet. Then again, if William had not dated in a good while as he said, they would have no idea other than maybe the couple had been dating for even years by now. Knowing this larger than life man as she was beginning to know him; he probably had just blurted out the truth to his children. He was very blunt in everything that he did. If he had not told them yet, then he was most surely going to tell his children that he and Lyla were getting married at tonight's dinner. Lyla was getting very nervous.

Lyla had a great fear when it came to telling her own children. She knew that she must tell them this week. She was not sure if she had to tell them about the marriage just yet, but she knew that she must tell them about moving. Gee, she had not even told them that she was dating William, much less the move. Her children had helped place her where they believed she should be. Telling them was going to be a very difficult thing to do. However, tonight was at hand. She realized she must deal with one group of children at a time. Both were making her very nervous. No date had been mentioned about a wedding as of yet.

William acted as though he was completely happy. He acted as though he had been planning this marriage forever and he was in complete control. That part of William bugged Lyla. He was always so much in control. Where was that going to leave her in the future? This was often just a passing thought, but for a second or so this worried Lyla. She guessed maybe she was just a little jealous because she wished she could be more like that.

On this warm Friday evening, Lyla spent much time getting dressed. She wanted so to look perfect for William's children. Luckily she only owned a few gowns. Therefore the choice in clothing was slim. Had she owned more she could have spent hours trying to decide what to wear. She worked and worked on her makeup and her hair. She prayed that she would be what the children would approve of for their father.

As the children of this powerful man started to arrive with their partners, Lyla was a nervous wreck. A beautiful young woman came in first. She was dressed in a pretty black gown that touched the floor as she walked. Beside of her walked a tall young man whom Lyla felt looked snobby, or to rephrase that in her mind. She thought,

"A Bit Stuffy!"

The young woman was most charming. She walked straight through the foyer, swung open a set of pocket doors that lead into the dining room and went straight to her father. She spread her arms wide open and hugged him tightly. She said,

"Hello Daddy! So glad you invited us to dinner!"

Lyla could tell right away she was going to like this pretty girl.

William turned to Lyla, who was standing by his side and said,

"Camellia, I would like you to meet Lyla."
Lyla knew from the look on the young lady's face that she had not been told one thing about her.
She softened her shocked look and said,

"So-o-o nice to meet you Lyla! This is my husband Scott!"
Well, the ice was broken on that introduction. Now Lyla braced herself for more. She heard the front door open and she heard the butler when he asked if he could take the next couple's things. Camellia and her husband had left the large doors wide open. There would be no surprise meetings tonight. She would know when someone walked into the house.

Secondly, in came William Jenson, Jr. He and his wife were dressed beautifully. The young William had his father's good looks. He was married to a pretty blonde that did not look that unlike a famous movie star. During their introduction, Lyla was relieved to find that this charming young man had not only his father's good looks; but he also had his charming personality. Before William could finish his statement of,

"*Will*, this is Lyla!"
The young man stepped over and gave her a big hug. Looks can be deceiving, because the pretty blonde named Joy was just as pleasant as her husband. She smiled largely when she shook hands with Lyla. Lyla was beginning to feel more comfortable. Then another daughter and her husband came in. This daughter looked much like her father and that made her very beautiful. Her husband was somewhat unusual with not much of a personality at all. The first words out of his

211

mouth were to a servant standing nearby. He bluntly said,

"Could you get me a Scotch on the rocks, ole' boy?"

His name was Chad and the daughter's name was Mildred. She was cordial enough, but she would give Lyla some fairly cold stares. Luckily, William had talked enough about his children to where Lyla knew that Mildred was the one who was the most rigid. These three children still had a living mother. The ex-wife was always disapproving of anything that William would do. Obviously her daughter was of the same temperament.

Finally, Louise and her husband Sam arrived with the other son, Jonathon and his girlfriend Sally. Louise and Jonathon were William's youngest children. They were by his second wife Sofia. Now, thanks to a store clerk, she knew that the second wife had passed away. Lyla was really nervous about meeting these children. This was because she knew after a tragedy of loss of a mother; no one could ever be good enough to marry their father. Her fears seemed to be unfounded. These beautiful children were extremely friendly and so very nice. Both smiled largely while giving Lyla big hugs. They must also have the personality and temperament of their father. They were acting as though Lyla had been there all along and as if this was her place to be. She felt most welcomed by these lovely children.

Much conversation was had as everyone took their proper places at the table. Lyla could not help but be in amazement when she found that little printed name tags had been placed upon each person's plate. She expected to be seated next to William but saw that her name tag was on the opposite end of the table. She had a funny thought of,

"Just like Ma and Pa!"

She found all of this to be most formal for one's family of children. Then again, dinners were always very formal around this place. Everyone dressed to the nines for each and every dinner. Lyla liked that. She thought it was very elegant for one to dress for dinner. She hoped that practice would never change. Candles were always lit. Beautiful cut flowers always adored the table. Lyla got back into her safety zone when she thought,

"Lord, I would not want the floral bill around here!"

Cut flowers seemed to be everywhere throughout the house. The beautiful flowers that were placed in her mother's room everyday were so appreciated. She laughed at her thoughts. She was forever thinking of how she would not want to have to pay for all the things that she was enjoying. She _could not_ pay for the things that she was enjoying! These people acted as if this was the most common of practices. They were so comfortable in this world that seemed to be about a million miles away from the ways of people like Lyla. She could not understand that either. She had always felt that she could hob knob with the very best of them. She could, but this was different now. This was up close and personal. William was going to make her one of _them_. She wondered if from that station; could she even fit in? She felt shaky inside. Was she doing a charade or could she really fit into this wealthy family? Would her more common side start showing shortly? Yet, she knew that she was not expected to put on or pretend to be something that she was not. So far she seemed to fit in quite well just by being herself.

Lyla only knew that she had never been this close to anyone who was as rich as this family. Oh maybe so; but in a different atmosphere, not in their homes. Now, while facing these children, she felt that she was masquerading as a wife to be of a multimillionaire. Funny thing though, this was not just a thought, she was not masquerading! She really was going to be the wife of a multimillionaire. When she put it like that, it even shocked her.

Lyla prayed that she would make the best of impressions on William's children. She prayed that she would do or say nothing that William would not be proud of. She knew that she must calm down and go to her professional side. She always knew that when in doubt, she should go to that professional side whether it was a bit stuffy or not. She knew how to play that part very well. Actually over the years that side had become a very large part of her. Suddenly, she became a nervous wreck again! Why? She was professional. She had to forget that she was going to be William's wife right now, just for this evening. She must show nothing but her professional side. This side she was very comfortable with while in large gatherings. It finally worked and Lyla was able to become more comfortable.

Dinner moved along smoothly. The family was served veal this evening. The cooks at this mansion were fabulous. The steamed vegetables melted in your mouth. There was a soufflé made in Heaven and so many wonderful things to eat. Tonight the dinner wine was wonderful once more, but before anyone was to leave the table, William had asked for Champagne. Lyla knew why and she was feeling the pressure of what was about to happen. How would this now calm pretty family react to the sudden moves of their father, William?

Jokes were made about being offered Champagne. Jonathon laughed as he looked at Lyla and said,

"Well, it is not Christmas. It is not any of our birthdays. No one is having a baby as far as I know. So, it must be something else!"
Everyone got quiet. Lyla felt tightness come into her stomach. She stared at William. Could he get this over with already? William was taking forever. He seemed to be toying with his children.

Camellia, who was sitting next to her father, reached over and put her hand upon his arm. She laughed and said,

"Come on Daddy. Spit it out. Who's pregnant? Is it Buster Shyllia?"
Lyla laughed under her breath. She knew that to be one of William's prized race horses. Surely this family did not break out the champagne and complete a dinner such as tonight for an announcement about a horse? Then she stopped and thought with a smile that (yes)! Yes, she realized that they probably did just that. She knew there was so much she was going to have to get used to and to learn about this bunch of charming people.

The longer the questions went on, the more nervous Lyla became. She could see the twinkling in William's eyes. He would look over at her and wink every so often. He was really enjoying the suspense of it all. He was really enjoying his children. She was so happy to see this loving exchange that William and his children were enjoying. He obviously had a close relationship with his children and this pleased Lyla. He seemed to be a wonderful father. She could tell that William was much loved by his children and she could tell that he loved them all very much.

Finally, all glasses were poured and William raised his glass for the toast. He said,

"I would like to make a toast to all of my wonderful children, without whom I would have never wanted to live. You bring me great joy and I love all of you very much. To your good health!"
Glasses clanged and everyone had a very big smile upon their faces. Then William stood up and raised his glass high up into the air. This time he said,

"This toast is to the lovely Miss Lyla! A woman whom I have come to love very deeply! To the woman I plan on spending the rest of my life with!"
Everyone got really quiet. Their eyes got big and all were planted directly at Lyla. They all looked shocked. Actually they looked very shocked. No one raised their glasses. Now, Lyla wanted to crawl under something or leave the room completely. She wished she could become invisible and just disappear. Just then Louise said,

"Daddy, are you saying you two are getting married? Or are you just wanting to shack up like so many of your age did back in your day?"

Louise had felt the tension and was trying to remove it from the room with laughter. She had said that all with laughter and the whole room laughed with her, but Lyla thought she could feel a big chill. William threw his head back and laughed at his daughter. Everything seemed to be all in fun when he said,

"Well daughter of mine, what do you think we should do? What do you think would be the most e-x-c-i-t-i-n-g? What would you do if you were we?"

Louise was laughing happily now, when she said,

"Oh Daddy, just tell us!"

So William stood up, raised his glass once more and said,

"Ladies and gentleman: This *is* an announcement! I have asked the lovely Miss Lyla to marry me and she has said YES!"

Jonathon had a large smile upon his face when he raised his glass and said,

"To Lyla!"

Everyone put their glasses together with a large clang and now that it was soaking in, all seemed to be very happy about the announcement. That was all except the daughter Mildred. She had toasted with her glass, but she was looking somewhat disturbed when she said,

"Little soon, isn't it Dad? How long have you two known each other?"

Lyla was stressed and decided this was a question that William was going to have to answer, however he seemed to ignore it completely. This man was so very good at that! If he did not like the question, he just ignored it and never answered.

217

Lyla knew how frustrating this could be. She felt sorry for Mildred when she did not get an answer to her question. So, she looked at Mildred and smiled. Then she said,

"For a while Mildred! We have been dating for quite a while now. Your father traveled through my town a lot this past year and we have dated for a while!"

This seemed to satisfy Mildred and the party went on while everyone was joking and carrying on. Now she was going to worry as to whether she would ever be able to win any compassion from this daughter. She also knew in her heart that yes, it was a little more than soon. It was, by anyone's standards, way too soon!

Lyla noticed that even though Mildred had joined in the fun of the evening, she was troubled and concerned. She noticed that Mildred looked at her wedding finger more than once. She thought that maybe she would just keep her mouth shut and wait for the next question. If she answered the question that she knew the daughter wanted to ask, then that would be too forward and she knew that. So, she decided she would wait and tell Mildred that her father had not purchased the rings yet but it was on his agenda. He had given Lyla a beautiful diamond bracelet instead and planned on the couple having matching wedding bands. There would be no engagement ring.

With all of the quick glances in the direction of Lyla, she finally decided to try to make friends with Mildred. She walked over to the fireplace where the lovely girl was standing with her sisters. This was a golden opportunity to make all of the girls more comfortable. She said,

"Look what your father gave me as an engagement gift."

All of the girls smiled. To Lyla's surprise, Mildred spoke up first. She said,

"Oh, that is just lovely!"

Each daughter chimed in with,

"That is so pretty!"

Or,

"I did not know Daddy had that good of taste in jewelry! It is a wonder he did not give you something designed like a horse shoe nail or something!"

All laughed. They all seemed happy while smiling brightly. Lyla knew that she had broken the ice and she was feeling so much better now. She complimented each of the girls on their attire and their beauty. She also told them how wonderful she believed their father to be. Then she added,

"Unless you girls have something derogatory you would like to tell me about your father. Remember that I intend to marry the guy. If you do, tell me now. It is one of those need to know things!"

Everyone laughed again. Lyla knew that she was being invited into the deepest circle of this big loving family. William had been watching from across the room. Lyla could tell that he approved. He walked over to the women and said,

"Are my beautiful women talking about me?"

Louise said,

"Yes Daddy. We were about to tell Lyla about all of your faults, but we decided that you did not have any!"

William hugged his daughters and then he hugged

Lyla. He said as he looked deep into Lyla's eyes,

"I paid her to say that!"

Everyone was having such great fun this evening. Lyla was feeling most comfortable by now and she was beginning to feel that yes she could belong right here. Yes, she was starting to feel that she belonged in William's home. Yes, she belonged to William.

The evening was coming to a close. William spoke over everyone and said,

"There is someone else I want you'al to meet before you leave. Lyla's mother has come to live with us and she is unable to leave her room."

Everyone looked a little surprised, but by this point it was as if they were expecting about anything that their father may throw before them. So like good little children, each of them followed their father and Lyla up the long stairway.

The nurse was coming out of the mother's room. She saw the large group approaching and she said,

"She is awake and I think she feels pretty good tonight. She ate all of her dinner. I was proud of her!"

Lyla knocked on the door and she could hear her mother say joyfully,

"Come in!"

The large crowd entered the room. Lyla's mother sat up high on her pillows. Lyla knew that her mother would be happy that she had put on the beautiful yellow dressing jacket that was purchased for her last week. She looked pretty in her yellow silk jacket while sitting in the middle of that big yellow bed. William spoke first. He said,

"Momma, I would like for you to meet my children."

Lyla was taken aback! She did not know that William had started calling her mother Momma! That was okay! It just surprised her. Momma was used much in the south. Lyla had always called her mother mom, mommy at times, but never mamma. Her mother did not seem to mind. As a matter of fact she acted as though this was most common. Of course Lyla did not know how many times William visited with her mother. She was finding out that he did that a lot. He seemed to enjoy her mother's company so very much. Lyla was happy about that.

After each child and their partners names were given, Lyla's mother smiled and said,

"It is so very nice to meet all of you. You all are so very beautiful. Just like your father!"

Everyone had big smiles upon their faces except for the one son-in-law who seemed to not care for much of anything except his Scotch. Tonight this family was getting acquainted and everyone seemed happy to do so.

Everyone walked out of the room but Lyla and she asked her mother what she thought of William's children. Her mom said,

"They are all so beautiful!"

Lyla told her mom that she agreed with her and she too believed each and every one of them to be beautiful just like their daddy. Then her mother got a real serious look on her face when she said,

"You know it will not be this easy with your also beautiful children, don't you?"

Lyla just shook her head in agreement. No, it would not be that easy with her children. She knew that her children would not approve. She remembered her daughter saying at the time that her husband had passed away,

"Now, all we have to do is to keep mother from marrying again!"

She knew that they would not approve of the move and now she must face them with the news of a marriage. Since nothing had been said about a date, hopefully she had awhile to prepare for that meeting. She was going to have to hurry and tell them about the move before one of them called one of the house phones back home and finds that they have been disconnected. Thankfully, they most usually called her on her cell phone. This also made her thankful that she had provided a cell phone for her mother ages ago. Her only salvation was going to be that after seeing this place she knew that her children would definitely approve of it for a home for her mother.

Lyla went downstairs to tell the children goodbye. She told each of them of how happy she was to meet them. Everyone smiled at her and said the same. The evening was over. William closed the door. Then he took Lyla into his arms. He said,

"Thank You!"

She said,

"For What?"

He said,

"For being wonderful and accepting my children as you did. I think they all like you very much."

Then he added with a chuckle,

"Even Mildred!"

Chapter 16

Lyla knew after the evening with the guests that she would most likely sleep like a log this night. She and William sat by the fire for a while before turning in. She was sleeping in William's masculine bedroom tonight, she realized that when he took her by the hand and lead her to his room. William had asked her on the day that she moved in if she wanted to keep her separate bedroom or did she want him to redecorate his and her move in with him. He gave her other choices as well like; just pick out another room completely.

Lyla actually loved her room and she hated his. The suggestion of moving in with him was completely off the table. The man actually had deer horns hanging on his dark wood walls. Trophies and banners were everywhere. Big, overstuffed leather furniture overpowered this very dark colored room. In one large corner stood a stuffed bear! The man even had black sheets. She had laughed when she answered his question with an 'it did not matter'. Then she had quickly added that they could be together, whenever and in whatever room they wished. She also told him that they both had too much stuff to merge it all together. Somewhere down the line after their marriage they could remodel and make adjoining suites, but for now things were just fine the way they were. Besides, she knew that there were times that both of them enjoyed their own space and their own time. Many nights they may sleep alone. This seemed to be perfect for this aging set in their ways couple. They both seemed to think with this plan the arrangement would probably make their relationship more stable. Amazingly they both quickly seemed to agree on that.

After the love making, Lyla fell asleep in William's arms. She had never dreamed of Flossy Mae when she slept with William. In a silly mood one time she had thought of how funny it would be to tell William about her many lives she had lived, and to tell him that right now he really had two women wrapped up into one. She would laugh at herself and say,

"What man would not be happy about that?"
Of course she knew that she could never share such things with William. So tonight, even in a dream state, she remembered being surprised when Flossy Mae came through once more. This time Flossy Mae was standing alongside of Rosalie at a funeral. Somehow, Lyla knew who had died. Rosalie & Flossy Mae looked so sad. These women looked as though they were probably in their late fifties now. Lyla could see Flossy Mae's reflection in the glass of a large painting hanging over the casket. Flossy Mae and her tight skinned oval shaped face still looked young. Her hair was graying, but she was still very beautiful. Both women were dressed in black and both were very distraught.

Lyla knew almost immediately that she was attending the Colonel's funeral. She could feel complete sadness surround her. She was feeling the pain and she was hurting beyond belief. A white handkerchief in her hands was soaking wet. A large crowd was standing by. Lyla was surprised that Flossy Mae was permitted to stand where she was. She was right alongside of the

Colonel's wife and their daughter Louise. Stranger still was that her own children were standing directly behind their mother. She realized that what was not to be known in life was certainly obvious to the world in death. After Jenny was raped possibly the whole community learned of the Colonial's other family. Lyla did not know. Flossy Mae had never shown her those in-between times. From the vision she was looking at right now, this was a family. The children were all much older now. Everything showed that this was a family of grieving mothers and their grieving children.

Now the vision moved to the gravesite. At one point, Flossy Mae and Rosalie hugged. Times must have really changed since the day that Rosalie had felt so superior. Now, large groups of people were coming up and hugging or shaking hands with Rosalie. Lyla noted that there still were very strong stations in this life of long ago. Flossy Mae knew that she must show her respect and stand back as a slave. She and her children moved further from the gravesite while all family and friends paid their respects to the widow and the daughter Louise.

Back at the house, Flossy Mae went into the kitchen. She helped the others prepare the massive amount of food that was brought to the house by so many family and friends. The large rooms all around the seating room were full. That room looked as if not one more person could fit into it. No matter what the community now knew or believed about this family, no one would ever admit that they knew such things. Some may feel compassion for the slave woman and her children but they knew that they must not show this compassion in public from fear of ridicule by others. Flossy Mae knew that she must regain her composure and pretend that she was only a saddened slave who cared about her master. She could never let it show that she was dying inside. She could never let it show that she had just lost the man that she loved with all of her heart, the father of her children and the love of her life.

The aging women knew the whole truth. Rosalie had learned the truth several years ago. She had found her husband's hand written 'Will' while looking for some odd papers in his desk. She was shocked and quite mad over what she read.   The Colonial had weeks of nothing but screaming from his wife. As sick as she had been, she certainly came alive when she realized that her husband had been with his slave woman for years upon years. She blew up and told him that he must sell Flossy Mae. She screamed that she wanted all of the half breed children gone and out of her site as well. Of course the powerful Colonel Winthrop Wayne would never agree to such ramblings on. Only time had calmed the situation. Rosalie finally realized that she could not change her husband's ideas or his 'Will'. She knew that he was too powerful and too strong for any of that.

In his 'Will', the Colonial had enclosed papers that freed all of his children and Flossy Mae. He had also provided for each and every one of them. He had large amounts of money set aside for each of them. He had given them complete use of the west wing of his mansion for the rest of their days. This was a wonderful jester, but Flossy Mae still worried. To this date, none of the children had married or anything. What were they to do?

They actually did not belong anywhere. They were not black and they were not white. Neither race wanted anything to do with them as far as relationships were concerned. It saddened Flossy Mae to know in her heart that they were to be alone for the rest of their lives. They would live in luxury, but they would be alone. Flossy Mae and Rosalie knew that the whole community now most likely knew of their family connection. They were determined to never confirm that idea. They also knew that no one would ever admit that they knew the truth. No one would ever say a thing about it. Even if there were whispers, the Colonel was respected way too much in his community for anyone to say anything against him.

On this sad day, Flossy Mae was appreciative of the house slaves when each one of them hugged her and her children and told them of how sorry they were for their loss. The children had now been told by this time about their father. He had told them himself several years before his death. They were able to become very close to the Colonel after Rosalie was the wiser. The other slaves had guessed. Everyone standing in that kitchen this day knew that Flossy Mae and her children had just lost a valued family member. Flossy Mae was grieving very uncontrollably, but she could not help but feel really sorry for the very stiff Rosalie. She realized that she had come to love the master lady too over the years. Rosalie had accepted all facts over the years and seemed to interact and care for the Colonial's other children. She was family as well. She knew that Rosalie's pride was also most likely killing her. She had to save face no matter what. For years now and still important was the fact that everyone must pretend that nothing such as this slave family even existed.

Flossy Mae did not have to work anymore if she did not want too. The 'Will' stated that she was completely free. She had her own money and she had a large suite for all of her comforts. But, she had sat down with Rosalie while the Colonel was in his sick bed. She knew that the proud woman must save some of her pride. The proud woman needed to save face due to her husband and his other family. The women had decided to drop all of their differences or at least hide them. Flossy Mae told Rosalie that she would carry on as she always had if it was her desire. She would remain a servant at the large home. She had said,

"What else could I do? I know nothing else. I will continue with my duties!"
Rosalie had agreed and the two women tried to get along. There would always be that master slave relationship underneath. Rosalie would always be mad over what had happened, but she had softened much over the past years and showed that she felt much of the reason the Colonel and Flossy Mae had become lovers was a blame she could claim to be her own. Flossy Mae was to realize that this woman also loved the Colonel very much and she respected that.

Lyla awakened and went to the bathroom. As she looked for her slippers she realized that she was not in her own room. She slide her feet into the very large slippers beneath the bed. Quietly she slipped into the bathroom trying not to awaken William. She stayed in there for a while as she tried to clear her head. Why had Flossy Mae showed her the funeral? What was her previous personal soul trying to tell her about the modern day? She knew that it would come in time but right now it seemed that she was living two lives. Living in this mansion as she did now only made the two lives more alike. This seemed to make the two lives merge in together in some way. Even her precious real life somehow felt like a dream at times. Her thoughts rushed wildly as she sneaked back into the bed.

When Lyla awakened the following morning she found that William had already left to do chores, so she would imagine. She lay there for a while looking at her surroundings and being thankful that she had not chosen to stay in this room completely. It was nice, but oh so very man cave like. Finally she let her feet hit the floor. She realized that she must borrow one of William's robes or put the clothes back on that she had on last night, because she had brought nothing else to William's room. She decided to borrow a big shirt that William had thrown over a chair. She knew that it should be in the dirty clothes, therefore he would not mind her using it.

The bed was so large and it had been sort of dark in the room when she went to the bathroom shortly after awakening. Before Lyla left the room she looked back to see a card and a long stemmed red rose on the pillow next to hers. She smelled the rose. It smelled wonderful on this Saturday morning. She opened the beautiful card. It said,

"I love you Miss Lyla. Thank you for agreeing to be my wife!"

Lyla smiled and held the card close to her heart. She just about jumped out of her skin when she reached over to pick up the rose though. Because, out of the corner of her eyes she saw that bear. Would she ever get used to that thing? She grabbed the pretty rose and down the hall she went while hoping not to be seen. Even in this large house there seemed to be maids and servants everywhere. She would have to ask sometime just how many there really were, because she felt everywhere you walked you almost stepped on one. She knew her flippant thoughts were only because she was embarrassed to be leaving William's room in his shirt! A lady in a grey dress and a white apron passed her and spoke. Lyla thought of how she really was going to have to learn these people's names. She knew that she must write them down. Just before she reached her room another lady walked up to her and said,

"Miss Lyla, could I bring you some breakfast or would you wish to go downstairs?"
Lyla thought a minute and realized if she ate every time someone asked if they could serve her, she would end up fat as a pig. So she replied with,

"I'm not really hungry right now. I'll just raid the refrigerator later."
She laughed to herself when she realized what she had said. She most probably was not expected to ever see the refrigerator in this home. She got a big charge out of the fact that she thought that the Lord William most likely did not know what one looked like. Then she opened her door before she laughed in front of the woman's face. Nights with William always had that effect on her. She was always so full of fun and happiness on the following morning. She decided this morning that she was just going to let herself be happy. No more worry. No more wondering what could happen if she just let things happen. What if she just let herself be happy?

C hapter 17

Lyla was surprised one morning when she looked at the calendar to write down the date that her mother was to go to the hospital for tests. She spoke out loud and said,

"Gee Whiz, we have lived here seven months."

Then she chuckled while realizing how time gets away from you when you do not have a job. When one does not have to do anything such as a job, one does not really even know what day of the week it is. You do not have to look at a calendar to plan an event. One in her current position does not have to write on a calendar when this or that bill needs to be paid. All you have to do is remember loved ones birthdays and any other important dates to you. Time also goes faster when you are happy.

By now all of the children had been informed of the upcoming wedding. Lyla had finally bitten the bullet as one would say and called her children with the news. She was a coward just as she had been when she called them to tell them that she had moved in with William. She called them both times from her mother's room knowing that speaking back and forth with grandma would lighten their anger.

William and Lyla had decided to wait until pretty flowering weather to have their wedding. They had decided to have it on the grounds amongst the many gardens of their home. Lyla liked the sound of our home. William said that often. He said it so much to where she believed it anymore. She loved her new home. She loved her big handsome man and she loved this way of life. Nothing could be better. She was living a fairytale life. Often she felt like Cinderella and thought that she may wake up around midnight some night and everything, including William would be gone. But she could not be happier.

The wedding date had now been set for June the 15th. The couple had thought about later in the year with fall colors, but Lyla's mother was failing fast. They wished to have the wedding while she was still around to enjoy it. Lyla could feel the coldness from her own children but she was very happy that she had already sprung the surprise on them. She and William had visited each child at their homes by now. Everyone seemed to love William, but still they were stand offish with their mother. None of Lyla's children had visited her home and their grandmother to date. Lyla just knew they would approve and come around once they saw the beautiful place and saw how happy she and their grandmother were.

William traveled often for his business and he loved to travel just for fun as well. He and Lyla had been many wonderful places by now. Lyla had been happy with the way that her children had accepted William even though they were still somewhat cold towards their mother for making the decisions she was sure they believed to be nuts. Her daughter showed that she really liked William but still acted as if she was somewhat guarded against him, but an acceptance of a sort was there. Lyla could not help but compare her daughter and William's daughter Mildred. She guessed these two had to have proof that everything was going to be okay.

Another month passed and Lyla's sons had now visited the ranch on a holiday with their families and she noticed that they were quite impressed. They all left their children for spring break just as they had always done with their mother. At the end of spring break her daughter came to the ranch as well. Lyla's daughter had only shown up to stay a very brief time for the reason to pick up the grandchildren who had visited for a week. Her children had arrived for their spring break stay with their uncles. An arrangement had been made that she was the one to pick them all up. Her daughter almost never left her room other than to go to her grandmother's room or to go to dinner. Her true feelings towards her mother about William, the house or anything else were hard to read. Lyla knew that it would take some getting used to the idea for her sweet daughter. Her daughter and William's daughter Mildred seemed to share in their standoff feelings for the new groom or the new bride. Both kept that guarded protection ring around them. That could not be bad. It only showed that they were strong and yes, protective of their loved ones.

Lyla did realize that all of the others, grandchildren included, were most impressed by the house, the property and William. Lyla's children were most thankful that this larger than life man would take such wonderful care of their precious grandmother. They thanked him over and over for that jester. William would only say that he felt that was the least that he could do and tell them that he loved their grandmother very much. He seemed to be most happy to have Lyla's children at his home. Whether they all were impressed or not, William was quite impressed by her children and grandchildren. He told Lyla after the first visit that her children were also very beautiful and he had taken notice of how intelligent they each seemed to be. This made Lyla proud.

As summer moved on, the couple had enjoyed more times with their grandchildren. Merging their families together caused one large group. As Lyla would watch her grandchildren ride horses or maybe play a video game with William's grandchildren, she was happy about that old saying of how children always seem to adjust. That statement was most surely true. If only the adults could just learn from the children? All of the grandkids acted as though they had been cousins all of their lives. Their acceptance of being a family was most reassuring to both Lyla and William.

Lyla was getting closer to William's family. Two of the daughters wanted to help plan the wedding and she had agreed. Finally Mildred reluctantly went along on a shopping spree to find a wedding dress. Lyla knew that she was only along because the other two sisters had insisted sternly. Yet the day ended up being much fun. The group of women went to a nice restaurant to eat lunch and all had a great time.

Lyla could not get over the high end bridal shops that the girls had taken her to. These shops did not carry a dress under ten thousand dollars. Lyla thought of how a wedding dress was probably a wasteful usage of money. They cost so terribly much to be worn just one time! She knew that William had plenty of money to throw around, but why would he want her to spend that much on a dress that she could only wear one time. Besides, the colored ones were even more expensive than the while ones. Lyla had decided on a yellow dress. Finally, after going through every shop in the local area, the ladies decided that it was time to go to New York. There they were sure to find the perfect dress. Lyla was in sort of a shock at this suggestion!

Lyla could not believe the things that could be done with so much money. The decisions that she considered to be snap decisions on William's part must just be the way of the rich. A person can obviously handle anything and everything in a spare minute if one has enough money. Almost with no time to think for Lyla, the girls had ordered tickets by computer for the whole group. Someone hollered,

"What's your daughter's phone number?" Unbeknownst to Lyla, the girls were inviting her to go along. Lyla wondered if her working daughter could drop everything and come along as the other girls had requested. But, this would be such a nice treat to have her loving daughter help the group pick out everything. She always welcomed any time she could spend with her daughter and an added visit would be such a blessing. Lyla heard someone say amongst all of the excitement and the noise of the girls giggling and making plans, that her daughter was able to join the group. The new bride was watching while everyone was getting so very excited to plan such an event. Everyone got involved. They were on a plane the very next morning on their way to shop in New York City. Her daughter was to meet them at the airport in New York. The Jenson girls treated this shopping spree the very same as Lyla would have considered getting into her car and driving across town to a mall.

The group was going to make a two day trip out of this venture. The daughters made all of the plans. They had made all plane reservations, booked a top notch hotel with each having their own separate room, and someone had booked a play for the evening that they would be spending in New York. All of this was done immediately after the decision was made. All plans were completed within one hour. Lyla was truly impressed. She did not have to do a thing but sit back and watch miracles performed before her very eyes. These beautiful young ladies were most diffidently their father's daughters!.

The trip to New York was wonderful even if Lyla did find it exhausting. She found out immediately that the Jenson girls loved to shop. They put a new meaning into that old saying, 'Shop Until You Drop!' This fit perfect with her daughter too, because she loved to shop as well. Lyla just smiled and shook her head (yes) at her daughter, when she saw her daughter pull out a credit card to pay for something she wanted only to hear Camellia say,

"Oh no, no you don't, Daddy is paying for this trip and our purchases. Daddy is paying for everything!"

The trip finally ended and Lyla was relieved when the ladies dropped her off at home. Her shopping was done and she was tired. She was so very tired!

The Jenson girls and her daughter had helped pick out the most perfect dress. Lyla would have believed this dress to be entirely over the top. She knew that it was way too expensive for her

236

blood, but she also figured that the girls knew what their daddy would like. She also knew that there was a proper face put on for the world to see in family's such as theirs. They must keep up tradition and airs in front of others. The dress was very beautiful and she felt like a princess when she put it on. She believed that she had never seen a prettier dress. Lyla was so full of love for these beautiful girls and she felt a new found relationship with her own daughter too. It was as if Mildred had accepted her now and Lyla's daughter Geneva had accepted the whole situation, the wedding and the new family. It seemed Jenny really liked William's girls and the beautiful model type dressy girl fit in so well. All of these young ladies were absolutely beautiful. Lyla always knew that her daughter was prettier than any movie star. She had found William's daughters to be the same. One can only imagine the impression these four girls all together made on the people in New York City. All beautiful, all with southern accents, every hair in place, all tall and thin and all dressed in the best and latest of fashions. She had noticed that one taxi cab driver could not take his eyes off the mirror. She worried he may wreck because he acted star struck. All four girls had crowded in the back seat while giggling and squeezing in. From the front seat, Lyla was watching the driver and the road. He seemed to be only watching the beautiful giggling girls in that back seat.

Finally the time arrived for the wedding. William had taken care of most all of the planning except what Lyla had ask to do. She had made all of the arrangements for her family and all plane tickets were purchased and paid for. Lyla had purchased a beautiful dress for her mother while she was in New York. She had helped pick out the dresses and the flowers for each of the girls. They had to be special ordered. Lyla had since mailed her daughter's dress to her. All had agreed to be in the wedding. The sons and son-in-laws were to stand with William and he had taken care of all sizes and the ordering of the tuxes. The girls and Lyla had purchased the dresses for the two little granddaughters who would be in the wedding. One was his and one was hers. It was the same way with the little grandsons, one of his and one of hers. William was taking care of the tux wear for them.

Lyla smiled in disbelief when she heard that the tuxes were to be purchased. Never had it crossed anyone's mind in the Jenson family that those sorts of things could be rented. The invitations had been mailed by the massive amount of employees at the home and nothing seemed to be left to do now, but wait. Lyla refused to let herself wonder what their special day was going to cost. She was sure that she would be unable to wrap her mind around such a large amount like that anyway.

On the day of the wedding Lyla kept a look out of the windowed doors on the terrace. Her daughter was with her and helping her dress. This private time was valuable to both mother and daughter. Her daughter had talked briefly with her mother and had asked if William made her happy. She had answered,

"Yes! Very much so!"
Her daughter had said,

"That's all I want to know mother. The most important thing to me has always been that, and I hope you know that. I want you to be happy!"

She hugged her daughter tightly and both tried not to shed any tears. They both said they could feel them coming up under their eyelids. Tears were not acceptable after all of that expensive makeup put on them by very highly paid professionals.

As Lyla and her daughter looked out over the fast filling back yard, they wondered as to just how many more quests would arrive. Lyla realized she had not asked how many invitations were sent out. She and her daughter both thought that they had never seen more people attending one event. Large white tents seemed to be everywhere. White chairs with what looked like from the distance, ribbons flowing from them, were lined up row after row. Lyla's nerves were becoming shattered. She looked at her daughter and said,

"It's a lot of commotion for an older lady like me, wouldn't you say?"

Her daughter hugged her again and said,

"You're not old mother. Actually you are very beautiful. Look at yourself in the mirror. You look just like a fairy princess in that almost millions of dollar dress! William wants it all to be so perfect for you. He must love you very much mother!"

Lyla looked at her daughter and said,

"You are right Darling. I know he loves me very much and I love him completely."

Then she blurted out,

"How much do you think this dress cost? Before I had it off my body in the dressing room, it was already paid for. I tried to find tags but they must not do that in that high class store. I have heard if you have to ask the price of something you

239

must not be able to afford it. Did you hear the price?"

Her daughter hugged her and said,

"Don't you worry about things like that mother! You don't have to worry about things like that anymore. You will never have to worry about things like that again! Do you understand that? I think your Mr. William may have more money than God!"

With that they walked down the hall to the mother/grandmother's room. They found her dressed and waiting with a large smile upon her face. She kissed her granddaughter and told Lyla that she looked absolutely beautiful. She kissed her granddaughter again and said,

"You look beautiful too doll face. But, then again, you always look beautiful. You are just too pretty my little angel."

Then she added,

"I just love things like this! I love weddings! Everybody looks so happy. It is going to be such a wonderful day!"

With that her aid pushed her chair to the waiting elevator. Lyla thought of how amazing even that was. William had installed an elevator so it could accommodate her mother's needs. How many men would do something like that?

As the mother went down the aisle with her aid to be seated in the front, Lyla and her daughter awaited their instructions from the wedding planners. A stern lady kept them hid behind the curtains of a small tent that had been prepared for the waiting bride. Lyla was hoping that they would not have to stay in there long. It was already feeling quite hot even with the fans that were placed about. She really did not want any of

240

that expensive make-up that took all morning to do to go down the tubes. She was fascinated with that. She could not get over the amount of people hired just for her, her mother and all of the daughters. She had never had anyone else put her makeup on. She really thought that jester to be stupid but had agreed after much pressure from one of the daughters. Now she was not sorry that she had agreed. The makeup people were experts. They did a wonderful job. Lyla felt she had never looked prettier and she felt the experts had taken ten years off her face. Maybe she should have them come to the house more regularly. They had the money. Then she laughed at herself while thinking,

"Just because you look like a princess does not mean that you are a princess!"

Lyla could hear the beautiful music playing. Her daughter and William's daughters had left the tent now and they were now walking down the aisle. She wanted to look out to see them do this because she felt that they all looked so very beautiful, but the lady in front of her motioned for her to stay back. Then she heard the wedding march start to play. She knew she must be ready. The stern looking lady looked out and then back in, then she looked out again then motioned for her to go.

As Lyla walked down the aisle to her waiting handsome husband-to-be; she could not have been happier. Every fiber in her body was saying,

"This is it Lyla. You've met him! You have met another man of your dreams. Pinch yourself to be sure that this is real."

241

Silly as that may sound, the charming lady took her right hand and pinched the forearm on the left. She was not taking any chances. When the pinch hurt, she said to herself,

"You *will* be happy for the rest of your days in the loving arms of Mr. William T. Jenson!"

Lyla had what she called normal beliefs. She also was so bad at picking any happiness she had to pieces. Did she feel that she did not deserve happiness or what? So in her normal character, thoughts crossed her mind on her long walk down the aisle. One such thought was of how the odds of someone her age ever getting married again were almost zero. She of course knew there were a few factors that played into this scenario. Lyla had never lost her perfect shape. She was able to keep her long blonde hair without looking like a silly old woman and she had wrinkled only barely throughout the years. She could still pass for a woman in her thirties.

As Lyla walked down the aisle, she was thinking of how she felt her world had ended with the death of her late husband. He would have never approved of this. Of that she was sure. He was much too jealous for that. Maybe these facts were the facts that made her question everything with William. She knew that she was feeling in some way that she was being untrue to her late husband. She had tried and hoped that over these years she had somehow dealt with those feelings. Now she must look to the future. Her husband was gone and she was about to embark upon an adventure with a new one. She could only pray that this journey would be as happy as the last one. Then the doubting Lyla thought,

"What are the odds of that, I wonder?"

How could Lyla ever be so lucky as to find love again? How could this be happening to someone who was so very sure that her life was over! She had even told herself that she had moved back home to prepare to die. She felt she must make her funeral arrangements and stay in her home area to lessen the burden placed upon her children until the final days arrived. Meeting William had changed all of that. Now today was her wedding day. This was as if she was given a second chance and a new lease on life. She was feeling completely blessed on this day.

William had planned the most lovely fairytale wedding. He would ask for Lyla's advice on certain things, but knowing she did not have the funds to afford a wedding such as he would wish, she stood back and let him take charge of the whole ordeal. The flowers were absolutely beautiful. William had spared no expense on decorations. Actually he had spared no expense on anything. The sun was shining beautiful rays through the trees and the flowers for this very special day. Lyla looked out over the crowd to see women with pretty big hats upon their heads just everywhere in the large gathering. This was the way of the south. This was the elegancy so much of the rest of the world had forgotten. This was the elegancy Lyla wished the whole world still had. Today this plantation looked more like the grounds of a castle and the wedding looked like it was arranged for royalty. She chuckled at her thoughts and said to herself,

"There you go again Miss Flossy Mae. We are Lyla today and this is a ranch!"

Lyla looked to the right and saw her pretty family. What they were missing in these deep
243

southern styles was only the hats. They were dressed beautifully and they were such good looking people to where they would have been beautiful in anything they could have worn. Lyla felt pride swell up in her throat with the love and admiration she felt for each and every member of her loving family.

As Lyla came closer to William, she could see the pretty smile he was wearing plastered firmly upon his face. He too was very happy and she knew it. She saw the complete satisfaction upon his face as he looked at her in her pretty gown. This is one day she could read his eyes and they were saying that she looked like the prettiest woman he had ever laid eyes upon. She somehow knew exactly what he was thinking as she floated down the aisle. It was as if they were on the same wave link or something. She was also thinking of how he was the most handsome man she had ever laid eyes on.

Lyla approached the large arch that was built for this very special occasion. Magnolia blossoms were attached amongst the ivy. White streamer ribbons and baby's breath bunches were scattered and attached throughout the arrangement, and they were blowing in the wind. The beautiful arch looked as if it were an eight foot floral arrangement. Lyla believed she had never seen anything so beautiful. Looking to her left she could see what looked like a million white balloons being held down high up between two trees by a netting of some sort. She watched William the whole time while she was walking down the aisle. She was very sure there had never been a man more handsome. She melted at the site of him. He had on an extremely elegant tux. His beautiful hair had been styled perfectly. This extremely handsome man looked beyond handsome today. In her exciting childlike mood, she giggled inside at the thought of how she sure was using the word extreme a lot today. Wonder Way? Once again this fairytale felt as though this had to be some kind of a dream.

"No one is really that good looking." Thought Lyla!

Lyla was walking alone today. Her father had been gone for years. Since this was not a first marriage for either, and for other reasons like she had not consulted her children about this wedding before accepting William's proposal; she felt she would be pushing their feelings should she have ask a son to walk her down the aisle. However, she had been pleasantly surprised when her daughter had volunteered to be her maid of honor and when her sons agreed to stand with the other men alongside of William. All of the children, hers and William's, looked so very beautiful this day. The rows of these *more* than beautiful people standing up in front, dressed in their beautiful dresses and tuxes made this day seem even more like a fairytale. She knew she was not exaggerating when she thought of how she had never seen anyone dressed more wonderful or faces more beautiful even in movies.

Lyla laughed at her own thoughts when she looked down at the huge ballroom type gown that she was wearing. There would not have been any room for anyone to walk alongside her anyway. The full dress with the hoop under the skirt took up the whole walk aisle. The large bouquet got in the way as well. It was full of big magnolia blossoms, white lilies and baby's breath. Lyla had

245

helped pick it out, but looking down at its size, she had to wonder about the things that money could afford. The flowers were wet, thus making her white gloves moist. She could feel the weight of this heavy bouquet. She had heard enough about the beautiful magnolia to know that if you touched its white pedals they would become tainted. She sure did not want to get to the front and find she had nothing but tainted magnolias with the color of dark grey or black flowers, so she held tightly to the arrangement and tried hard not to move them. Realities such as this kept her grounded so that she would not once more feel like she had just walked out of an old movie or a fairytale. Everything was just too wonderful, seemingly too good to be true and so very romantic!

Then, as if the clouds opened up, the whole world changed. Lyla's eyes got big and she almost went into shock. Oh God, this wedding was not real. Her relationship was not real. She was not where she thought she was. She really had not seen a Shaman who told her that she was sane. She was in a dream state. There was no William. There was no mansion. She was more than likely in a hospital somewhere and she had really lost her mind. The Shaman she had conjured up was more than likely her psychologist. The large buildings of a mental hospital could make ones dreams be that of mansions. *She knew it! She just knew it*! Nothing could be as she was experiencing today. It was way too wonderful. No human could ever experience such a thing in this life time. She felt her heart breaking and oh so hurt when she started to believe it had all been just a dream. Now it was all coming down around her. Why was she waking up? Why not at least let her finish this wonderful dream. How cruel of a Lord or a bad brain cell. Why could she not stay in that beautiful state forever in the safety of William T. Jenson's large loving arms?

Lyla almost tripped over her large dress. It sure seemed real enough and it was still there. She watched her handsome husband-to-be in the distance. Everything became a blur. She thought she was going to faint and prayed that she would not. If there remained a possibility that she was in a real world, she must continue as if she was. If she was not; well then someone would surely come and get her and take her back to her quarters and maybe give her a pill for being so crazy. She had always felt if someone fainted at their own wedding it could be construed to mean that the person was having second thoughts about the marriage. But in Lyla's case it was so much more!

There before Lyla was the handsome man she wanted to marry. He was changing! His clothes were morphing right before her very eyes. She watched as his beautiful black tux jacket changed into an off beige color. The front of the jacket lengthened and a wide belt was placed over top. The tails seemed to be getting longer. Before her _stood_ the very same man with his broad shoulders and extreme good looks, but suddenly he had a beard. Lyla, in this mental state could not understand why her silly mind would want to change such a vision of loveliness? To her the man she had dreamed up had been perfect. So perfect to where he had to be what she had always wanted, but how could she be able to rationalize things if she was crazy? Well, she had never been crazy before so maybe this is just the way it is.

Lyla's William now had on a tall black hat that looked not unlike those she had seen in pictures of Abraham Lincoln. His beautiful white, black and silvery hair was long. The waves were deep upon his head while they showed ever so neatly below the tall hat. William's coat was now very long. As Lyla let her eyes slide down his body she saw that the coat came down longer in the back and was now touching the back of his knees. Upon this coat was a braiding of some sorts. The pants had a satin looking stripe that now went down the side of them and they were stuffed deep down into tall black boots made of leather. A long brocade case was attached to that wide belt upon the long jacket that fell below the knees. It held a long sparkling sword. Lyla almost fainted.

Suddenly, Lyla did trip badly enough to where she had to catch her flowers before they hit the ground. Her thumb pinched a large pedal of a big beautiful magnolia bloom and it instantly turned dark. She thought,

"Oh No! A tainted magnolia! Please, Dear God, don't let this be a sign of any more bad luck!"

She twisted her ankle in this little act and then she knew for sure that this whole ordeal was real. It all was so very real and happening right now! She was not losing her mind, but instead she was seeing things that she should not be able to see. Why her? How do things like this happen to normal people? She could only believe that the whole crowd was now in total shock, however she looked out over the crowd and everyone was still watching her march down the long pathway with great big approving smiles upon their faces. Was she the only person seeing what was happening? Was this just a bride's wedding day jitters?

Lyla tried to cover the ordeal and kept walking ever so gracefully. Dear God, this was not a dream! She was not crazy. She knew something was crazy, but obviously it was not her and she was really where she thought that she was. This was something that was happening in real time. This was something so much bigger than her or all of the people around her. Something very strange was happening at her beautiful wedding and she did not think she appreciated the intrusion. Suddenly it was as if someone slapped her in the face with reality. She recognized that large man standing before her now as someone other than her love, William T. Jenson. *M y   G o d*, *My God,* she was looking into the face of none other than the ***C o l o n e l   W I n t h r o p   W a y n e***. He was there in flesh and blood, standing strong with all of his power and his oh so good looks. Good Lord, this was him! She had seen him so plainly in dreams or visions given to her by Flossy Mae. Yet she had not remembered details of his face nor how very good looking this man really was. The metals that hung from the lapels of his jacket were catching the sunlight and they were shining brightly. Nothing could look more real. The man was *really* there on this day. Now she was starting to understand the ever presence of the Flossy Mae dreams. She now knew why everything had gone as it had. All of a sudden she realized why she and William felt like they had always been together. She knew now why things had moved so fast between them. This was their destiny. They were marrying their soul mates. They were extremely happy, but now she knew that neither of them had

249

any choice in the matter. They were preordained to be together for eternity!

Lyla knew that Colonel Wayne was dressed in full uniform for this very special wedding. A more handsome site she had never seen. Even though she had got small glances at the man's face before in her dreams, none of those visions seemed to stick. Flossy Mae had neglected to tell her that this man was so extremely handsome. Lyla had never seen such a man before meeting her love William T. Jenson. She believed that probably no one could ever say the word **no** to such a person. William demanded that very same massive presence. In the military attire there could be no larger presence than the *Colonel Winthrop Wayne* was showing! Oh the massive power that this man was giving off this day.

Lyla looked down at her own attire and found that her dress had changed in color. It was now of a white linen. The skirt seemed even larger than it had been before. The material was now all bunched up all over the skirt and a small bow was tucked at the ending of each bunch. She imagined there were hundreds of bows upon this beautiful dress. It felt very heavy. She felt a large wiring or maybe a wooden type unit beneath the dress that was holding it far away from her feet. She could feel the ribbons of her long bloomers. She knew this was real. She could not imagine how, but she knew this was all too very real. The Colonel and Flossy Mae were getting married this day. She had a hurtful thought of,

"Strange, I thought William and I were getting married today! But who is?"

Lyla had believed that her dress of yellow to be the prettiest dress she had ever seen and she felt like a princess in it. But at this very minute she knew she was in another of the prettiest dresses anyone had ever made. She looked down at her hands and noticed that they had changed colors as well. She could see the beautiful bronze color of her skin and she knew at this very minute that she was no longer Lyla. She was now Flossy Mae.

Why were the guests acting as though nothing strange was happening? They were all smiling and watching her walk down the aisle as if everything was quite normal. Lyla thought of how if it were she in the audience, she would have run screaming or fainted dead away when people morphed right in front of her. Then she realized that no one else was seeing this. Possibly not even William, but how could that be? Maybe he too had visions or dreams he had not shared with her. Maybe he too felt that she would believe him to be crazy should he share such things with her. She could not help but wonder if William was totally aware of what was going on. She knew that she was now Flossy Mae! Surely she was not the only person at this wedding who was witnessing this unbelievable scene! Now, she really did feel just like an actress in a play.

Lyla suddenly realized that the strong and powerful Colonel Wayne was correcting all of the wrongs of his previous life. She knew that he was making it *right* with Flossy Mae. Lyla thought silently,

"My God, he did love her!"

Lyla had often hated the Colonel in her dreams. She could not believe the treatment he had given poor Flossy Mae. Today, she suddenly realized that he was a victim of his times just the same as Flossy Mae had been. It may have taken centuries, but this strong man was going to correct all of the mistakes of the past and he was going to marry his beloved Flossy Mae. Unbeknownst to his modern day self, William, this was the one and the only woman he had ever truly loved. He had loved Rosalie, but that was in a different way. His heart and his soul belonged to Flossy Mae from that day when they were only children underneath that old magnolia tree.

This all was so strange to Lyla knowing that possibly William and for sure the entire group of people who were surrounding them, were completely unaware of any of this. She knew that she must act as normal as possible. In her mind's eye she was jumping from one scene to the other. However, she somehow knew that the crowd and maybe even William were staying in this day and time. Once upon a time she would have believed that she was going completely mad. She still felt that way many times. Even today up until she tripped a ways back, she was writing herself off as certifiably insane. Lyla thought of how dreams and visions while she was alone and asleep was one thing, but these happenings were most definitely insane. Broad daylight, no sleeping and on the happiest day of her life she is seeing dead people all around her. In a way she wished that the large group of people attending her wedding could witness such a thing. How nice it would be to witness an undying love such as this. A love that had lived through the centuries! A love that would never die! But, she knew no one would understand. She also knew that they all were so not aware of the amount of love around them on this day!

With the slow walk down the remainder of the beautiful aisle, Lyla knew that there were two people within her at this minute and she was much aware of them both. William was changing back and forth in the other dimension just as she. Suddenly upon the approach to the handsome groom, William was back. Lyla looked down and saw that she was once more herself. That was not to last. When Lyla placed her hand into William's, they changed again into the Colonel and Flossy Mae. It was as if the Colonel Wayne and Flossy Mae were the only people in this yard this day. Even the scenery had changed. The grounds no longer looked like the grounds of the ranch. Lyla glanced back at the house and saw that it was no longer William's, but instead it was the very same beautiful old home that she had seen in Louisiana. She smiled and whispered a thank you, hoping Flossy Mae could hear her. She was thankful to Flossy Mae for allowing her to see the beauty of that old home in the days when it was still standing properly and proud. It was so very beautiful with the tall pillars all around it. Lyla looked to her left and she saw the largest and the most beautiful Magnolia tree she had ever seen. It was in full bloom. It looked as if someone had decorated it like a flower arrangement while placing each and every large bloom in the most perfect of places. She had not noticed this tree before and knew most if it was not really on the Jenson Ranch? The trunk of this tree looked like it was about five feet across. As if Flossy Mae was answering her questions in her mind, she knew immediately that this was the tree Flossy Mae had told her so much about. This old tree had been there on the day of the Colonel and Flossy Mae's youth. This old tree

253

had been there the day she was caught hugging Samson. This old tree knew it all and it had been invited to the wedding on this day. Looking again, she was sure it was not really there. She knew in her heart that this was the tree from the Wayne plantation. This was the tree that Flossy Mae and the Colonel frolicked around so many, many years ago.

Cold chills went down Lyla's spine. Dear God, her husband to be *is* none other than the Colonel Winthrop Wayne. She was so very sure of that now. Why did he not know the Colonel? Why did he not know that he was him? Why was he not seeing the same things that she was seeing? Then again maybe he knows and sees but was feared of telling her. Maybe he is seeing the exact things that she is seeing right now. If so they must surely think much alike because he too is doing a marvelous job of keeping his composure. A bigger question came to Lyla's mind,

"Why had she not suspected this before while learning of so many of William's ways and manners?"

Now she knew why they had always felt as if they belonged together; *they truly did*! Now she knew why she had no say in the matter. *She didn't*! Now she knew when she had tried to rationalize everything and tried so hard to not jump into these things so hastily, she now knew the reasons she could never say no to the large and in charge Mr. William T Jenson. She found relief when she could guess that William did not have any say when it came to decisions made about her either. Now she understood everything! Now she knew it all!

Lyla had tried to talk to William about this before. She would always stop short of the story. She felt many times that she should maybe tell him. She did not want to start their life out with secrets. Yet, she did not want her future husband to believe that she was completely crazy. She felt certain he would want rid of her if she told him the crazy things that happened to her. So she walked lightly with the subject. She tried to get into the depths of his mind. She tried to discuss his beliefs, but when she would ask,

"Do you believe in reincarnation?"
He would always snap at her with an answer like,

"Read your Bible! It is appointed unto man once to die!"

That statement was in the Bible. No one knew that scripture better than Lyla. This one statement had closed so many people's mind to anything different. This one statement had closed William's mind to any other possibilities. Lyla had been taught that the Bible was 100% true in every way. The only justification poor Lyla could give herself in this situation was that maybe that statement meant something else other than the strong headed way everyone seemed to read it. She knew the Bible was true. She also knew what she had seen was true and real. Believing what she had seen to be a lie would cause her to have to believe that she was completely insane. She preferred to believe otherwise. There were too many unanswered questions and unexplained happenings for any of this to be a figment of one's imagination. This fact made her believe once again that possibly William did not have any idea that he was the Colonel Winthrop Wayne. Just as her life in the Victorian era, William may never know he had lived before because he possibly had a closed door to that subject.

Lyla knew her Bible well and she was a firm believer in God, but there was nothing narrow-minded about her. She knew that King James had picked and chosen what he wanted in his Bible. She also knew there was much more information out there that had been ignored over the years. The difference between her and most other people was that she always kept her mind completely open. She always was willing to listen to all possibilities. She knew in her heart there were millions of things that a mere human mind could never comprehend or could ever understand. She knew there was a large universe out there and she had always been so hungry for knowledge. She was open and she was free in her way of thinking. She was sure that is why Flossy Mae came to her so freely.

Lyla was again sure that she was right back where she started. She knew that she could not talk to anyone about her feelings, beliefs or these happenings in her life. She often felt so alone! If she ever even mentioned such things to others they would look at her as if she had completely lost her mind. Only the Shaman in Alaska had understood. Had it not been for her, Lyla is sure she too would have also believed that she was losing her mind. She would have started to believe that Flossy Mae was a figment of her imagination. In her heart she always knew better than that. The feelings were too real. The visions were too real. There were too many things that had happened that could not be explained in anyway other than the fact that Flossy Mae had come to visit.

Nothing could ever explain away the experiences with the houses in Louisiana. Nothing could be more real than Lyla's views into Flossy Mae's life. When one can feel the cool rocks beneath one's feet or the blades of dew covered grass wiping across your face. There is no explanation for these kinds of things short of reincarnation. Lyla had accepted Flossy Mae into her life to where she felt her to be as much a part of her life as the current entity Lyla.

Lyla figured William was maybe too dogmatic in his thought process to ever see anything except what he had been taught. Maybe his strong belief system would not and could not be shaken. In reality Lyla admired him for that. She loved his strong will and his comfort in his beliefs. She knew that he somehow felt that if he believed in reincarnation that would cause him to lose his faith in God. With what little amount of discussion Lyla had with William regarding this subject she knew that he feared he would not go to Heaven with such beliefs.

There were times Lyla had questioned reincarnation as well. These were the reasons for so much dismay when Flossy Mae was trying to contact her. She now felt there was nothing further from the truth, but she was not going to try to change William. Strangely, Lyla now felt the opposite. She felt that reincarnation reinforced her belief in God. There were so many things in one's life they would never be able to understand and she did not claim to have all of the answers. She felt she had been blessed with a knowledge that others were possibly not allowed to receive. Most others would never know these things. Yet, she often wondered why. Why was she given this
257

blessing? Maybe it was not a blessing at all. Maybe it was a curse or a burden that she would have to bear for the rest of her days. She could not help but wonder how many others shared in this blessing or cruse; whatever it may be and she wished she knew others with these experiences!

As the long dress dragged across the wide mat that had been rolled out over the grass, Lyla found herself to be in another world. It was as if time had reversed and she had just walked down an aisle at another plantation during the 1800's. She was there! William was there! Everything had suddenly become different.

This event could have never happened for Flossy Mae. Flossy Mae had traveled over the years to be here today. Those things that are, can be very strange. Lyla had felt Flossy Mae's presence so strongly today even before the wedding. Once today while the lady at the spa was putting on her make-up, Lyla looked into the mirror and instead of seeing herself, she saw Flossy Mae. It was a shock at first, but being so used to the presence of Flossy Mae, Lyla had laughed and said under her breath,

"Are you enjoying this professional makeup job they are doing on us today? You do know that they are doing your makeup as well as mine, don't you?"

Lyla then laughed at herself for being so silly, jittery and giggly today. But she knew that never had Flossy Mae come through so plain. She also knew Flossy Mae had never visited during the day while she was awake. Another very strange thing was that today Flossy Mae was saying nothing and there seemed to not be a story to tell on this day. Flossy Mae had always come to Lyla when she was asleep or in a sleepy state. She had always had a story to tell. Lyla knew that these times were the only times her brain was calm enough for Flossy Mae to come through. That theory had just been shot down, because there she was on the most special day of her life. He brain was anything but calm today.

Lyla believed the reason most people do not understand or see the things that she sees is because life and problems get in the way. One's mind is so full of their daily lives to where there is no room for anything spiritual. She also believes had her family not had the ESP gift and had she not lost her husband as she did, she too would have never been able to see such things. She imagined that the hurt and the time she had spent alone were probably factors in her being shown her past. She had become strong enough through her grief to be accepted or channeled into the spiritual world. But today was proving there to be other reasons.

Now, on this fairytale day of Lyla's dreams, she was wondering what kind of life she was going to have with William. She realized quickly that this was not even something of their choosing. Could she and William have stopped their marriage or relationship had they so desired? It was becoming very obvious that today was Colonel Wayne and Flossy Mae's union. This was their destiny! William and Lyla were but vessels to carry out that destiny! Somewhere inside, Lyla knew this was William and her destiny as well. That only opened up a much larger can of worms such as; why had she and William not met when they were young? Why were others allowed to be married to each of them? There were at this point more questions than answers. William loved her and she knew that she loved him. She had never in all of her years felt more love and so much like she belonged. Both she and William belonged in this relationship. She knew no matter what her fears; their marriage could be nothing but long and happy.

Lyla knew she would have to think this entire thing out at a later date. Right now there was a wedding going on. Just as sudden of change as before, once again the wedding seemed to be in the 21st century. As the pretty bride came closer to the Reverend and the man of her dreams, she watched as William changed from William into Colonel Winthrop Wayne and then back again to William. It was now happening so quickly before her very eyes to where she was getting dizzy. The rest of the ceremony was as if it were in a haze. Just as the minister started to say,

"I now pronounce you man and wife." Everything got even weirder for Lyla. Suddenly it was as if the couples separated from each other. Lyla looked beside of her and there stood the ever beautiful Flossy Mae in her beautiful gown. She looked down to see her own lovely yellow gown back in place upon her body. Her hands were once more a pearly white color. She looked up and saw the ever handsome William T. Jenson facing her with the warmest smile she had ever seen. She could see so much love in his eyes, those same eyes that she could not read before. Obviously William could let his soul show on demand.

Flossy Mae looked at Lyla and smiled the sweetest smile. Lyla knew that she was saying thanks. In a flash, the Colonel Winthrop Wayne showed up directly beside of William while he faced the lovely Flossy Mae. He too had the same wonderful loving look upon his face. Lyla wondered why or how all four of them could be showing up at the same time. She and William were standing the closest to the minister while the Colonel and Flossy Mae were in line with them closer to the audience. As she looked at William, the Colonel and Flossy Mae she thought of how wonderful this event truly was. All were holding hands and showing true complete love for each other. The minister was telling each of them that he was now pronouncing them man a wife. Lyla thought of how he should have said,

"I now pronounce you husbands and wives."

Of course that may not have been proper either since in reality they were only two people. They had just stretched their lives over a couple of a hundred years!

Lyla took a closer look at Flossy Mae because it was as if the lady was in a real body now while standing next to her on this day. She noticed that the face looked exactly like hers and the contour was exactly the same as hers. The only difference was that Flossy Mae was black and she was white. Lyla suddenly felt the largest wave of love go through her veins. A warmer feeling she had ever felt. It was as if the whole world was nothing but love. She knew that she would never be able to explain the love she felt surrounding her on this day. She realized this wedding was a planned double wedding. It was for both she and Flossy Mae.

Lyla and the Shaman had believed that Flossy Mae was coming through for a warning of some sort for Lyla, but maybe the wedding was why Flossy Mae had come through to her so clearly. She must have been only waiting until the day when she could be married. If there would be a next time Flossy Mae would come to her she would try to ask that question. Lyla felt a relief. If she could contribute the visits from a two hundred some year old lady wanting to wed, then she would forever be okay. Just maybe Flossy Mae was not coming through into this life to warn her of some un-foretold danger. Maybe she was there so that she and the Colonel could get married. But a thought crossed Lyla's mind of how Flossy Mae also wanted her to know all of the bad things. For some reason of doom maybe, who knows. All the new Mrs. Jenson knew was if there was any other reason for Flossy Mae's visits, well then she would just think of them on some other day. No worries about letting Flossy Mae in. She would always be welcome in her heart. Today was filled with complete happiness for both she and Flossy Mae

When the Reverend said,

"You may now kiss your bride!"

Lyla felt William's arms come around her ever so tightly. Out of the corner of her eye she could see the Colonel take Flossy May into his loving arms. A warm blissful feeling flooded through every vein of Lyla's body. This was her wedding day but this was also Flossy Mae's. A horrible wrong had been made right on this day. The blissfulness of this day was to live on forever! A verse from the Bible came to Lyla when she thought,

"On earth as it is in Heaven!'

At this very moment, William took Lyla's hand and they walked briskly back down the aisle while everyone was throwing rice upon them. Lyla looked up as the many balloons were

262

released. Maybe the other couple left with the balloons to their home on high. The Colonel and Flossy Mae had disappeared. They were nowhere to be seen at this time. Lyla felt a loss. It was as if she had lost a big part of herself. She somehow knew that Flossy Mae and the Colonel had completely disappeared. They seemed to be nowhere around. However, she was so very happy for the Mr. and Mrs. Colonel Wayne, just as she was for the Mr. and Mrs. William T. Jenson.

There was a passing sad thought without a goodbye for Lyla, but she had other thoughts of how that was okay too! Flossy Mae was now leaving her to her own happy life. Lyla was not sure of how she knew that Flossy Mae was gone for good now from her life, but she knew that she could rest in peace The world now belonged to only William and Lyla. The grounds went back to the modern day Jenson's yard. The big old Magnolia tree disappeared and the sun was shining brighter than Lyla could ever remember! Someone up there was making very sure that this was the most beautiful of all days!

As at every large wedding, pictures were taken everywhere and with everyone. As the couple arrived inside of the big ballroom, the band was already playing. William took Lyla into his arms and the handsome couple floated across the ballroom floor. Lyla felt saddened that Flossy Mae had left so abruptly. She too would have enjoyed this wonderful party. Unlike the party that she had shown Lyla from her past. At this party she could have danced along with everyone else. In Lyla's heart she knew that the Colonel and Flossy Mae were off somewhere in the clouds enjoying their own love while allowing Lyla to have her very own special day amongst the living.

Lyla knew as William held her tight that she was not dreaming. She was not crazy! Two worlds had joined if only for a brief time to correct mistakes that society had made so many years ago. Lyla was happy she could have been a part of that. She felt blessed that she had been able to see things that no one else seemed to be able to see. For the first time since standing along that roadside in Louisiana, Lyla was happy for her experience. She smiled and squeezed her husband's hand while thinking of what a lovely day this has been! Lyla had just married her soul mate. Life was grand! Lyla's life was now so very, very grand! Now she knew that she would be so completely happy forever and always!

Lyla and Flossy Mae's life does not stop here. Read the book

ꞌConflictꞌ

for more of their story.

Books written by this author are sometimes written like a trilogy, or as in this case a second book was written with more about the same characters. The wonderful thing about this is that each book is a complete story. However, if you read one you will most definitely want to read them all.

OTHER BOOKS AVAILABLE BY THIS AUTHOR ARE:

Historical Fiction

The three first books could have been published as a trilogy called 'The Tragedies of the Dahl's'. These books chronicle the lives of three generations of the same family starting during the 1800's. A family named Dahl, an old farm house, a dirt road and the love of a good book has helped to inspire the rage and desire to write these very inspirable books.

Downloads and E-books are available:

To Order Books

Go to

Author's Storefront:

http://www.lulu.com/spotlight/litytarama

Author's webpages: www.marilynpavlovsky.com

www.book-burningsunshine.com

Books are also AVAILABLE @ Amazon and other sites were fine books are sold

CHILDREN'S BOOKS
AVAILABLE BY THIS AUTHOR

Telling the stories of life on a horse ranch and written as if the oldest Jack-Rat dog Trudy has written them, these stories are in rhyme. The author with the help of the fun things these animals do each day, created the *Trudy Books.* Trudy and the author tell fascinating stories about how she, her brother and sisters were rescued. She tells about her fifty or more horses and all of the other wonderful animals on her farm. More books are added to the author's web-site regularly.

THE TRUDY BOOKS are
Full of pictures – Fun for all ages
Available at the author's
Web-sites/storefront
www.marilynpavlovsky.com
www.book-burningsunshine.com
http://www.lulu.com/spotlight/litytarama